Mask of Sorrow

Mask of Sorrow

Laurie Brady

Mask of Sorrow

Mask of Sorrow
ISBN 978 1 76109 263 3
Copyright © text Laurie Brady 2022
Cover image: Asad Photo Maldives from Pexels

First published 2022 by
Ginninderra Press
PO Box 3461 Port Adelaide 5015
www.ginninderrapress.com.au

The sentence is that the individual shall throughout his life be
dragged to the place of execution. In other words,
remorse has become insane.
Kierkegaard, *The Concept of Dread*

Remorse is nothing but the wry face that a conscience makes
when it sees itself hideous.
Machado de Assis, *Epitaph of a Small Winner*

1

'What have we got, Ken?'

'Blonde female, twenty-seven, Mrs Lucy Grainger, knife wound to the upper body.'

'Perpetrator?'

'No. Long gone.'

'And the murder weapon?'

'Long gone too.'

'Who found the body?'

'Next-door neighbour. Mrs Chandler. Lois Chandler. That's her wrapped in a blanket over there. She's a real mess. Constable Harries is with her.'

'Are you OK? Is there something you're not telling me?'

'I'm all right. No two are ever the same, are they? I suppose there's always something in this job to challenge even the most hard-hearted of us.'

'Like what?'

'Well…she heard their dog, a golden Labrador, barking and whining, kept on and on around nine forty-five, so she went across, found the dog sitting in the open front doorway, blood all over its paws and snout, must have been licking the body, wondering why she wouldn't wake up and talk. It's way of getting help, I suppose.'

'Shit.'

'Yeah, anyway, she called, no answer, tried the door, it wasn't locked, went up the stairs, calling out as she went, scared as hell, found her in the bedroom on the floor.'

'Mrs Chandler can wait a little longer. Is there a husband?'

'Yes, an Ed Grainger. Neighbour says he's out Tuesday nights.'

'So he doesn't know yet?'

'No. It's some meeting he goes to, some historical society. She doesn't know what or where…no way of contacting him, but he'd have to be back soon.'

'Children?'

'No.'

'Is Doc inside?'

'Yeah.'

'I know how you feel about the dog…it probably knows, smells it. They must recognise death like we do.'

'Silly, I know. It's not the first body I've seen, but it broke me up.'

'Robbery gone wrong?'

'Probably not. The place hasn't been ransacked. No evidence of someone looking for something.'

'G'day, Doc.'

'It's pretty straightforward, Clive.'

'She hasn't been moved?'

'Not yet.'

'What can you tell us?'

'Early days. Single knife wound, at a guess at least a fifteen-centimetre blade, probably struck with some force, between the fourth and fifth intercostal, no sign of a struggle, no bruising or defensive wounds. Death would have been almost instantaneous.'

'Recent?'

'Two hours. Three at the most.'

'Sexual activity?'

'Doesn't appear to be. Not part of the crime anyway. Still fully clothed. I'll know more when I get her back to the lab.'

'Anything else?'

'From the position of the wound, probably a right-hander.'

'Well, that really narrows it down!'

'Thought you'd like that. The forensic team is already here.'

'Go and speak to Mrs Chandler, Ken. Wait. What the hell's the commotion! Why isn't the street cordoned off? We don't want every Tom, Dick and Harry having a look.'

'My guess is the husband's arrived home. Roberts must have let him through.'

*

'I'm sorry, sir, but you can't drive any further.' The young constable, too uncertain of himself to be officious, approached the car briskly with a torch and held it in the window.

'But I live here.'

'If you wouldn't mind leaving your car over there in Ridge Road, sir, I'll get someone to walk you to your house, as soon as…' Then seeing Ed's confusion, 'The street is a crime scene, sir.'

'But has someone…is that the house?'

Ed pointed at a two-storey Cape Cod in blond brick where three police cars were parked, two of them in the driveway. One had its high beam directed towards the house, illuminating the front of the lower storey and entrance. A rotating red light on top of one of the cars was muddying the lawn in rufous light.

'Is it, no, is it number seven?' He knew it was, it was his house, but shock seemed to cast a shadow on an awful reality.

The young constable, seeing Ed's reaction and suspecting his identity, asked him his name. There was no answer, but he didn't have to ask a second time.

'What's happened?' Ed whispered breathlessly, unable to move from the driver's seat. He felt anchored.

The constable looked at him sympathetically, not sure what to say next. Jeffries was inside. Perhaps he should let him know.

'What's happened?' Ed shouted, finding his voice as the implication of the police presence dawned. He wrestled with the door handle. 'Tell me! For God's sake, tell me,' and opening the door, he stumbled and fell onto the road, battling to regain his feet and rush to his house.

'Sir, I can't let you go charging over there. If you give me the keys, sir, I'll park your car over there near the kerb.' The young constable, who barely looked as if he'd begun to shave, was trying to do what his training had taught him. This was his first experience of something so momentous in police work, and he was feeling emotional.

'Is it Lucy?' Ed whimpered. Who else could it be? The significant police presence confirmed it, though he had been too shocked till now to ask for details. 'Is she, is she…?' He grasped the constable's arm and looked at him pleadingly, as though his mere intensity might change a terrible truth.

The constable eased the keys from his grasp, and moved to the driver's door. He was battling for self-possession himself. 'If I could ask you to stay right where you are, sir. Sergeant Jeffries will be with you right away,' and he looked towards the crime scene, hoping his sergeant would hurry and relieve him.

Ed took a few steps towards his house and halted. The constable had called him back. He was tempted to rush over. It was his house after all. He had every right to be involved with any crime committed against his wife or his property. Lucy was nowhere to be seen. She could only be inside. But he'd been given definite orders.

A procession of police, some sheathed in apple-green protective gowns and white footwear, entered and left by the brilliantly lit front door. Everything was silent except for the occasional murmuring or a barked instruction coming from inside the house. It seemed like a pantomime. Everyone seemed to know their part in the action. Ed felt heady with the sensation that he was both part of the action and a commentator on that action, first and third person.

The street was a short cul-de-sac, and people from nearly every house fronting the circular loop at the end of the street had gathered on their lawns to watch, most of them staring silently as if they were watching a peep show or a stoning. A few, like old Mrs Timmins, watched from behind the curtain of their bedroom windows, believing that respectability demanded less intrusive interest. Madge Turner watched openly from her porch, her bitterness with the world probably turning to glee when the possibility of someone's transgression had received a deserved punishment. Several children in pyjamas kept badgering their parents for explanations.

Ed could see Lois Chandler, his over-attentive neighbour, sitting on the garden bench he'd recently bought and placed under the front window near the roses. She was with a female officer, and wrapped in a blanket. While it was hard to see from such a distance, she seemed to be trembling, and taking in the scene of Ed's arrival.

As the young constable returned with his car keys, Honey, Ed's Labrador, rushed from Lois Chandler's grip and bounded across the road to meet him, nearly knocking him over in her attempt to get closer to him, pushing against his thigh and, with her head thrown back, howling like a coyote. She was trembling too. Dried blood had stiffened the fur a dark maroon around her paws.

'It is Mr Grainger, isn't it?' A voice reached him from some subterranean depth. He hadn't seen the man approach. 'Sergeant Jeffries. Clive Jeffries.'

Ed looked up, his eyes taking seconds to focus on a beefy man with the bare arms of a wrestler, hugged by the pale blue of a police shirt uniform. He had a pleasant face that wore a certain world-weariness but forbearance nonetheless, deep-set blue eyes beneath bushy blond eyebrows, and thinning sandy hair through which a pink scalp glistened. The Christian name was added as a personal touch to inspire confidence. Ed felt comfortable with him, if anything like comfort was possible under the circumstances.

'I'm sorry to keep you here,' he said. 'I hope you understand, but we can't have people traipsing around and ruining any possible evidence. And that goes for you, young lady,' he addressed Honey, a tactic to relieve tension, and patted her head, receiving a lick on the hand as acknowledgement.

'Is it...?' Ed queried, looking searchingly at Jeffries. There was no need to say any more.

It wasn't the first time Jeffries had broken the news to a spouse or parent. He still remembered his first time as a young probationary officer: a distraught pregnant woman whose husband had been attacked by drug-affected youths for no apparent reason beyond his being an easy target on a dark and deserted street late at night. He'd missed the last bus after a late meeting with interstate colleagues. She'd only been married a year, and it was her first child. He had held her, against all the advice of his training, found her strangely attractive beyond the lure that shared pain's antidote encouraged, and was zealous in tracking down the sixteen-year-olds responsible.

The years, all-too-frequent repetitions, and a word of advice from a wise senior officer, had taught him greater discipline and acceptance, though breaking the news to loved ones was always painful. He remembered them all, the hysterical, the silently stunned, and those battling to keep up the pretence of self-possession and see the tragedy with some shred of sense.

'Yes, I'm afraid it is. I'm really sorry. I can see you're in shock, but if you feel able to answer a few questions now, only a few, we can do the rest tomorrow.'

'But what? I mean, was it…?' Ed knew the answer. An accident would not bring this number of police, and suicide was out of the question.

'Yes, I'm afraid it was,' Jeffries pre-empted. 'The coroner and a forensic team are in there now. I'm not at liberty to give you details yet until the cause of death is established.' He saw the sudden look of horror on Ed's face, and realised he'd been too abrupt, running ahead of himself.

'We'll need you later to identify the body, Ed.' No matter how calming he tried to sound, it still felt harsh. 'I'm afraid there's not much doubt. She was still in possession of a driver's licence, and credit cards are in her wallet, and of course the pictures on the dresser.'

There were a few seconds of awkward silence as both men wondered what to say, Jeffries from sensitivity, and Ed from numbness.

'But was she…was she…and how…?' Ed's mind was chaotic, searching for a thread. Where to start?

'It's unlikely that she was sexually assaulted.' Jeffries intuited Ed's meaning, but avoided talk of how. 'It's small consolation, but I can tell you that she probably didn't suffer at all. Now, I think you'd better let me do my job,' he said kindly, 'and ask the questions.' So saying, he assumed his official role, though not without sensitivity.

'I have to ask this, Ed, but where were you tonight?' Jeffries's use of his Christian name made it seem less of an inquisition. Or was the personal touch a tactic he used to lure interviewees into a false sense of security before he pounced? The disguised simplicity of a Columbo.

'The History Club.' Ed's words were barely a murmur, faltering. 'It's at the community centre. I go every Tuesday. Mainly teachers, retirees.' He realised he had to be dismissed from the list of suspects. 'Tudor England tonight,' he said distractedly, Henry VIII and his wives, and the wives who…'

He stopped, seeing a trolley wheeled from his front door towards a white van. His voice broke and he couldn't continue. It was Lucy underneath that white shroud of sheets. He could see where her feet lifted the covering. Tears were running down his cheeks. He watched as the wheels of the trolley collapsed, and the bed it carried was slid into the back of the van.

Jeffries didn't press.

'Can I see her?' Ed asked haltingly.

'Not just yet,' Jeffries replied gently. 'You can see her when the autopsy is complete. I'm sorry, Ed,' he continued, 'but I also have to ask this. Was your marriage a happy one? Was there any conflict between you?'

'Very happy, very,' Ed answered instantly, and began to reconsider his earlier liking of Jeffries.

It was a ridiculous question. Who was going to answer that they hated each other and fought like cats and dogs? Even if true, and for him it wasn't, it would be tantamount to making yourself the prime suspect. He'd later wonder whether such an instant answer was too glib like the criticism Gertrude made in *Hamlet*'s play of the actor for protesting too much. Might it arouse suspicion, or did a more considered answer leave greater room for doubt? Perhaps there was method in the madness.

Jeffries was watching him closely, no doubt attuned to any little non-verbal signal in his face that could be a giveaway.

'Look, there's a lot more I have to ask, Ed, but I think you've been through enough for now. We can do it another time. We'll be here most of the night, I'm afraid. We can't let you back in just yet. Is there anywhere you can stay? Is there someone you'd like the constable to call?'

'I'll be all right,' Ed answered, not by any means certain that he would be. There wasn't anyone. He didn't know where his father was, and his mother had recently died. If only she'd been there for him now. He mightn't manage to drive anyway. 'The neighbours are kind.'

As Jeffries hurried away to be swamped by the attentions of other officers reporting on the tasks they'd been given, Ed suddenly felt dizzy and, aware of the sour taste in his mouth, crouched in the gutter and was sick.

The house was only fifty metres away, lit like a beacon, and Lucy had met her end in there. Would he ever be able to return there? What did she look like when Lois found her? He'd have to ask her. Did her eyes stay open, revealing the terror of her final moments? Did she die straight away, or did she bleed to death? 'Bled out,' wasn't that what they said on the crime thrillers? Jeffries had said that she didn't suffer, but he might say that anyway. He wouldn't say she spent her final minutes in agony.

He realised there was so much he hadn't been told. He thought of seeking out Jeffries and asking more questions. Surely, as husband to the deceased, he deserved that.

'Deceased'. 'Deceased'. What sort of word was that! 'De', removal of or from something. Removal from ceasing to be. Was it some technical euphemism to substitute for 'killed', 'murdered', 'annihilated'? What about 'butchered'? 'Bloody butchered' he felt like screaming at the ghouls who still watched, even though the numbers had thinned since the body had been taken away. What television were they missing to watch this production of *The Butchering of Lucy Grainger*? Was it *The Farmer Wants a Wife* or *Marriage at First Sight*?

'Ed.' It was Lois Channing from next door, a coat over her pyjamas. Her face was white, the lines deeply etched, and mascara had run. 'It was me…I was the one…' She'd stopped trembling, hovering between giving and receiving sympathy. 'It was Honey howling, a terrible…chilling sound…I went in…I hope you don't mind. I kept calling for Lucy, I knew something was wrong, but…' She needed to talk, but couldn't, and started to sob.

Ed waited, reaching out his hand, but it went unnoticed. Her face was buried in a handkerchief.

'I thought so…when I saw you sitting there with the officer,' he stammered, 'I thought you must have been the one…the one who… Is it real, Lois? Am I dreaming this?'

She stopped sobbing but was shivering from emotion rather than cold, and hugged him tightly, a shared need. The tears were rolling down her cheeks. He was dry-eyed and a ghostly grey-white. He wondered if he looked ethereal, insubstantial like a ghost is supposed to be. That's what he felt like. Floating.

They stayed like this for several minutes, clamped together.

'You know you can't go back in there, Ed. I don't suppose you're allowed to anyway. You're staying with us tonight, no arguments, and so is Honey.' Helplessness demanded direction. 'You can stay for as long as you like.'

*

He didn't want the television interview, but Jeffries insisted. It was the worst of reality television. Ed thought the overt and extravagant show of emotion even cheapened what he'd had with Lucy. Still have, he kept telling himself. The quality of his relationship with Lucy didn't have to be publicly demonstrated. He had nothing to prove.

Jeffries thought the interview might help. Television and news programs were thirsty for coverage. A puzzling murder of an attractive woman in one of the better suburbs, and one that carried the possibility of being a crime of passion, was enticing television fare.

'Someone out there probably knows something,' he told Ed. 'Any bit of information, however small, might be just what we need.'

'I don't want to make a spectacle of myself,' Ed replied, 'of Lucy or myself.'

'Ed, we need the public's support,' Jeffries insisted. 'Besides, there's nothing more appealing for the people out there,' he gave a sweeping gesture, 'than an impressive show of grief as evidence of your decency… your integrity.'

'What do you mean…a show of grief?' Ed protested. 'You're making it sound like a performance.'

'Sorry.' Jeffries hurried to right the implication. 'I didn't mean a performance. I meant for you to be yourself, to show what your wife meant to you.' He looked away and continued in a whisper, 'And what you've lost.'

So Ed was interviewed, refusing to whole-heartedly play the role of the bereft partner begging the public for information, and checking the tears when appealing to the murderer to do the right thing and confess. He spoke sparingly of his love for Lucy, leaving it to Jeffries to make the appeals to those who might know something.

The public was sympathetic to Ed, though a minority, given to egregious outpourings of grief in television viewing, believed he might have displayed a great deal more emotion when interviewed.

The press gave commiserating coverage, showing photographs of the house, and a stylish one of Lucy taken at a conference a few years earlier. It provided a sanitised account of the murder scene, and described the hardships of Ed's background that, to his displeasure, had been provided by a once-close school friend. This distant friend described him as a good student, a loyal son, perhaps something of a loner, and fond of intellectual pursuits rather than the rough and tumble of boys' games. He seemed to remember that Ed had been out with a few girls, but his first real girlfriend was Lucy, who he'd met some years after he'd left school.

*

Jeffries sat in his office with his feet on the desk, twisting a rubber band around his fingers as he read the autopsy report, stopping occasionally to read the more relevant parts to his colleagues Ken and Kane.

Growing up in the Sydney suburb of Drummoyne, Clive Jeffries always wanted to be a policeman, and laughed telling his colleagues that the idea began with a charismatic teacher telling the primary school children that law and order were the cornerstones of a healthy society. From that time, 'cops and robbers', with him as 'cop', was his preferred childhood game. He played the even-handed dispenser of justice.

While it wasn't his parents' preferred vocation for their son, they didn't stand in his way, and after leaving school, he trained at the police academy, and was appointed to a small station on the outskirts of Tamworth before being transferred to Sydney after two years of exemplary service.

He married Elizabeth at twenty-four, and she'd supported him through good times and bad, never complaining about the night shifts and weekends. She'd been a policeman's daughter and knew what to expect. They had two girls, Sarah and Imogen, both happily married.

'A single cut from left to right with a serrated knife that punctured the chest between the fourth and fifth intercostal. Definitely a right-handed murderer.' Just as Doc had predicted. 'No bruises or abrasions. No apparent struggle, which probably suggests the victim was approached from behind before turning round to be struck.' That was consistent with the position of the body. No recent sexual activity. No surprises. The time of death was between eight p.m. and nine p.m.

'Did you find the knife, Ken?' he asked his partner.

Ken Carpenter was a short wiry man, with a slim and lined face, receding forehead and wisps of mousy-coloured hair. He had a habit of pursing his lips when deliberating and speaking precisely. Not the typ-

17

ical image of the robust policeman, but he had a reputation for efficiency, and for leaving no detail unexplored. Meticulous.

When Clive had left Tamworth for a policing position in Sydney, Ken had followed. He was older than Clive, though junior in rank. His marriage had been short-lived and the divorce was acrimonious. His wife blamed the unrealistic demands of police work, though the real reason was the inability of both to share a common reality, to reach a workable understanding.

Clive thought the knife might either have been left at the scene of the crime, or dumped nearby. That was the usual pattern, particularly if the murders weren't premeditated.

'We've been over the house, the grounds, the dumpsters and drains with a fine-toothed comb,' Ken replied. 'Nothing.'

Every neighbour in the street had been interviewed and names recorded for later checks. Some were unnecessarily voluble, wanting to share their opinions. Others shirked any involvement and were even resentful of being seen with police at the door. One neighbour thought he'd heard a car driving away at speed around nine o'clock, but couldn't be certain of the time.

Most of them liked the Graingers, saw them as a pleasant couple who'd give a cheery hello when addressed but who kept to themselves. Some used the police presence as a chance to complain about others. Madge Turner confirmed her reputation for retailing gossip: 'the nasty man next door who dumps his rubbish over the fence' or 'the wild teenage parties with bottles and condoms left on the lawn'.

'I'll do the usual checks on the husband,' Ken continued.

'Yeah, do that, it has to be done, but I think we'll draw a blank there. Poor bugger.' He was thinking of Elizabeth, and Ed's conviction of his happy marriage.

'You've dismissed the idea that it was a burglary gone wrong?' Ken asked.

'It might have been,' Jeffries conceded. 'Nice house…someone looking for drug money. But something tells me otherwise. For instance, how did the murderer get in? There's no evidence of a break-in.' He sighed and placed his feet up on the desk once again. 'And then there's the lack of a struggle. Of course she might have been taken by surprise as the Doc seemed to suggest, but I think someone had been there with her for some time. Perhaps the interviews of her work colleagues will turn up something. We'll just keep digging.'

*

Ed stayed with Lois and Ted Channing for two nights, but felt the need to escape. He found Lois's unnecessary attentions suffocating. She was well-meaning, but asked too many questions. She might have thought it would do him good to talk about it, but he was never left alone to indulge his own grief, and thought she needed him more than he needed her.

At first he was concerned for the Chandlers because of the never-ending interruptions of the media, but when Lois protested at his departure, he realised she thrived on, and was invigorated by, the constant media interest. She was revelling in the role of a restoring angel, enjoying the public sainthood.

He moved to the nearby house of an old school friend who had left with his family for overseas the day after the murder. He could have gone back home. The police had finished their forensic examination, but he couldn't face the prospect of rattling around in the place where Lucy had met her end, the place that was no longer their haven. Not yet. Perhaps not ever.

His friend's house seemed large, too many rooms to be swallowed in. He slept for much of the day and night, the retreat of the depressed, hearing the crows from the unfamiliar bed, the mournful lament with its human sounding fall. A rooster crowed at first light from somewhere, bins were tossed noisily from a garbage truck, teenagers next door played loud music into the early morning hours, and above his head in the roof, beyond the bedroom ceiling's harsh hypnotic light, the possums scratched to tease his early morning images of Lucy.

If he ventured outside, the air seemed to weigh too much, and it was one more day to face an indifferent world, to brave the platitudes from well-meaning friends, to nurse the images of Lucy that intensified rather than diminished, and to hear the hollow voices that sounded as if they came from underwater caves.

2

Some people claim to have vivid memories of their very early years, even of being babes in arms. Ed doesn't. Most of his memories are fragments, struck matches in the dark, flaring for a moment and quickly extinguished.

From his infants' school years, he does remember playing catchings with a bean bag, a small and soft pouch-sized bag of beans that children threw to each other, probably to prevent the injuries a ball might cause, and to his horror, accidentally throwing it onto the school roof. He remembers sitting in a circle in the infants' school hall with very large workman-like boots, all painted a shiny red, yellow or blue, and the children using them to learn how to tie laces. He remembers being transported to different worlds when the teacher read the class a story. And he recalls sitting in the front seat of the classroom, eager to please and impress his teacher, a practice that continued throughout his school life.

As he entered primary school, he remembers his father calling him a 'home body'. He was pleased at the time. It seemed to suggest that he was a good helper for his mother, but in later years it took on a more pejorative meaning. Did it mean domesticated? Lacking in adventure or initiative like other boys? Perhaps lacking in colour? Was it a desirable thing to have, or the symptom of an insecurity?

As an adult, he'd still remember these early childhood days, picking the memories clean like pilling on a vest. Apart from school, all the world was home, a place you learned to eat and sleep and love, perhaps to die. Being anywhere else was beyond his understanding.

His enduring childhood images in the years before things were to so dramatically change, were of the Sunday family outings in the old Ford Prefect with the scent of chocolate from father's weekend surprise, chocolate he and his brother tried to leave unsucked on their tongues to make it last, chocolate that insinuated with the fragrance of his mother's lavender perfume.

His father, lean, with a shock of prematurely silver hair, and sparkling eyes, liked nothing better than these family outings, and would sing loudly and out-of-tune as he drove, at first provoking laughter before the pleas to stop. His mother, buxom, raven-haired and with a gentility that made her so softly spoken she was sometimes not heard, prided herself on the lunches or afternoon teas she packed. Todd, his brother, blond with a rash of freckles, the image of a television mischief-maker, was always restless, wanting to know when they'd arrive.

Ed recalls initialling the car's side window in the vapour caused by his breath, and watching the country hurtle by, all open vistas and a sky of softened blue that smiled on straw-coloured grass and grazing cows. He'd watch his father's long-lobed ears that hung beside the silver sprouting hairs on his neck, and feel strangely wakened to his fallibility, a feeling that became a tenderness for all the world, a feeling he was still too young to understand, and a feeling that disappeared when he left the car with its imposed complicities to squabble with Todd, and question the arbitrariness of adult law.

Those early primary school years were peaceful eternities, times to play in the cubby house, an old wooden packing case for a car that stood beside the paling fence between privets. It was a ship, plane and rocket that carried its all-conquering heroes to hostile worlds and returned them unscathed for mother's cup of tea and biscuits.

At weekends, he'd have to spend half a day helping his father in their constantly overgrown backyard, weeding the gardens. He thought it an imposition at the time, and only as an adult wondered if it achieved any useful purpose, but began to realise that apart from the help, it may have been a strategy of his father both to teach his boys responsibility, and his opportunity for communion with them.

Ed and Todd were required to do their homework after dinner in a downstairs converted tool room. Ed had an old kitchen table, and Todd, whose work was not as demanding, had a makeshift desk shelved with wooden fruit boxes, still labelled with supplier's names, in which he kept his textbooks and school equipment. The room was shut off from the other activities of the house, and there were frequent interruptions from the whining plumbing in the exposed overhead pipes.

The brothers slept in the same room, and before sleep overtook them, would improvise their own serials, though Ed would often get disturbed by Todd's fondness for the gruesome and violent deaths of virtually every character in his wild plots, and refuse to continue.

The room wasn't near the kitchen, but he could hear his mother at six a.m. preparing the porridge and setting out the breakfast things. It made little impression at the time, but in retrospect, he saw it as a symbol of security in those halcyon years. She never complained. Perhaps she understood that dogged love, dished out like cold apple pie or sausage sandwiches for school, would in the end suffice.

As an adult, it occurred to Ed that there may have been some meaning in the pullover colours that his mother lovingly knitted. His were blue and green. Todd's were red and yellow. Todd's colours were about passion and gaiety. His colours were more subdued, those of sobriety, perhaps conservatism. Was it a message about how his parents saw him?

There was a difference between them. He was the quieter and more introspective of the two. He liked the familiar and rarely questioned authority. He wasn't a risk-taker, liked established routines, and imposed a structure on his day-to-day life. Todd was the more adventurous, more chaotic, and was always testing himself against what the world and his older brother offered.

Ed recalled the time at Manly when he was nine and Todd was eight, and they were standing on a wall several metres above beach sand.

'Let's jump,' Todd urged, but Ed didn't want to.

He didn't feel comfortable with how high it was, or what was under the sand, and told his brother not to.

'Chicken,' Todd called him. 'I'm going to,' and he did.

Ed saw him grimace when he landed, and knew that he'd hurt himself. But Todd put on a brave face, and would not admit that he was in pain. He explained the limp he had for a few days on something altogether different.

A more memorable time was when they were shopping in Coles, and Todd saw a small toy he fancied. All these years later, Ed can't remember what it was.

'I'm going to pinch it,' he told Ed.

'But it's stealing.' Ed couldn't believe what he'd just heard. It was so wrong, and what would happen if they were caught?

'Don't be a sissy,' Todd said. 'And don't tell Mum and Dad. It'll be exciting. I want to see if I can. You can wait outside if you're worried. And if you're that much against it, we can come back tomorrow, and I'll put it back.'

He did take the toy, hiding it in his jacket pocket and walking casually through the checkout. He was delighted with his success. Ed can't remember if it was ever returned.

*

For the September school holidays, the family went to Forster, a thriving town on the north coast, four hours from Sydney. They spent most mornings swimming at Main Beach, returned to their rented cottage for lunch, and went exploring in the afternoons. They visited Seven Mile Beach one afternoon, and Cape Hawke Lookout in Booti Booti National Park on another afternoon, where they enjoyed the spectacular views and went on long walks through the surrounding rainforest. On the third day, they went whale watching with Amaroo Cruises. Ed recalls these early days of the Forster holiday as some of the most satisfying in his infants and primary school years.

The fifth afternoon remains rooted in his memory. His father went fishing, a pastime that was torture for the rest of the family, his father spending most of the time cursing and untangling lines, or snagging his finger on a fish hook, so they were spared the boredom of going with him.

His mother had seen a dress in a shop in the town, and after agonising over the cost, had decided to buy it. She rarely bought anything for herself. 'I'm not going to be long,' she told the boys. 'An hour or two at most. I want you to stay here. I won't be away long,' she said again. 'We can do something together when I return. You decide what. Ed, you're in charge. Watch your younger brother, and don't go getting into trouble.'

They played with their Lego for ten minutes before Todd announced that he was bored. 'Let's go to the beach again,' he said.

'No,' Ed answered. 'Mum said we have to stay here. You heard what she said. We'll do something when she comes back. We might be able to go to the beach then.'

'You're a spoilsport,' Todd taunted. 'You're no fun at all. Do you always have to do what people tell you?'

'No, but I think we should do what Mum tells us. If she comes home and we're not here, she'll be worried.'

But his brother's criticism hit a raw nerve. The impression that he was boring had recently come from a couple of mates. Quiet, dull, stay-at-home Ed. Todd continued to cajole, and Ed finally relented.

'We have to leave a note,' he explained, and scrawled a message, leaving it on the kitchen table.

He felt a little better when they arrived at the beach. It was mid-afternoon, and there were still a lot of people there, so there would be safety in numbers. It was hot and blue, and beyond the breaking waves, the ocean was a mass of crystals.

Todd threw his towel onto the sand, kicked off his thongs and charged towards the water.

'Between the flags,' Ed called after him, but even though Todd didn't hear him, he'd done the right thing for once and disappeared between the flags.

Ed was in no hurry. He lay his towel on the sand and spent a few minutes applying sunscreen. The sun was hot on his shoulders, and the beach was a feast of colour. He was about to follow Todd into the surf when whistles began to shrill, and three lifesavers plunged into the water and began to swim beyond the breaking waves. Two others stood knee-deep in the water at different ends of the flags with whistles, calling for swimmers to return to the beach. Two had already mounted jet skis that were slicing through the shoreline waves to open water.

Families sitting near Ed stood and craned their necks to see. They were worried, all speaking at once. 'What is it?' 'Do you think it's a shark?' 'Has someone drowned?' 'Oh my God, Jenny's in there.'

Ed tried to make sense of the jumble of comments.

'It's a rip,' he heard a voice say. The owner of the voice, a man burnt the colour of treacle and weather-beaten, was squinting out to sea. 'You can see them all being dragged out. Look.'

Ed and several others looked but things didn't seem much different. But a few swimmers were calling out for help or waving their arms.

Men, women and children were already being pulled to shore. There were many helping hands. A voice ordering swimmers from the water boomed over a loud speaker. The two jet skis had already completed their rescues and headed back to sea. A few rescued swimmers sat bent over on the beach spewing water as family or friends comforted them. One middle-aged woman was unconscious, and a lifesaver was performing CPR.

Ed felt sick.

'Thank God.' He heard a woman's voice find a place in his confused mind. 'It's Jenny, she's all right,' and he saw a man walking from the water with his arm around the shoulders of a skinny girl his own age. Ambulance sirens were already blaring.

Wrestling for composure, Ed ran to the water's edge, finding a space between the string of frightened watchers. A crowd was gathering, searching the waves for love ones. There was no sign of Todd.

'Please, please,' he muttered to no one in particular as he cried, and ran backwards and forwards along the shoreline.

Todd had started between the flags, but where might he…

A woman saw his distress and tried to comfort him, holding him for a few seconds against her ample bosom. 'Who's missing, love?' she asked.

'My br…brother,' Ed stammered, wrenched himself free and darted away.

He ran to see each person who was dragged to shore. An aged and bony man with the few remaining wisps of white hair glued to his scalp. A very large woman with one naked breast glaring from her costume. A girl his own age with water streaming from her mouth and nose, quickly enveloped by crying parents. A macho man arguing that he hadn't needed help – he could have saved himself.

The crowd was slow to thin. Some found their loved ones, an answer to prayer. Others were helped to ambulances to accompany their co-matose or dead to hospital. Still others were thirsty to view the human salvage. There was only an occasional rescue now and, once ashore, the bodies, mostly beyond further help, were quickly covered. There were four ambulances on the road and paramedics were working over pros-trate bodies.

Ed had stopped running along the shoreline. He stood stupefied, suddenly aware of his mother standing beside him. She had discovered their towels that were hanging on the line at the cottage were gone, so it wasn't hard for her to guess their movements. She hadn't gone inside so hadn't read the note.

And she didn't have to ask what had happened. She'd seen her fran-tic elder son running along the shoreline. Ed tried to say something to her but couldn't. His mother didn't speak at all, but looked out at the ocean with unseeing eyes.

Todd was the last to be brought to shore, lifted from a jet ski and carried to the water's edge. How long had it been? Twenty minutes? An hour? Two? How do you measure time? Does it move slower at a time like this? There was no rush now. The rescuer, a paunchy mature man in red and yellow lifesaving attire, seeing the look of recognition from Ed and his mother, glanced at them sorrowfully, and walked towards them slowly shaking his head.

Ed could see Todd's body in the man's arms, puny in death, his face bone-white with bluish lips. His mother saw it too and sank to her knees on the sand, making strangled animal noises that Ed would never forget.

*

For days, weeks, his parents said nothing. He wished they had. The silence was unnerving. It was torture. It would have been better if they'd stormed, shouted their condemnation, withdrawn privileges, spanked him.

Meals were silent. Harrowing. The tension was palpable, not only towards him, but between them. The warmth had gone from his mother. She'd say a curt goodnight when it was his bedtime, but she no longer came into his room to kiss him goodnight. He could hear his mother and father arguing in their bedroom next door, the soft, even voice of his mother, and the more excitable and accusing voice of his father, sprinkled with expletives.

Even at the tender age of ten, he knew what they were arguing about. His mother was defending him, probably admitting he'd been disobedient, but that he was suffering every bit as much as they were, and his father, less forgiving, was blaming him entirely for Todd's death, and wanting to punish him.

One night after a few weeks, when his mother did finally come to kiss him goodnight, he tried to apologise again. 'Mum, I'm so...'

'I know,' she said, and that was all, but she hugged him for a few seconds, patting his back.

He cried. It was the first affection she'd shown him.

Six weeks after the death of Todd, the silent war of attrition continued. They were at the dinner table having their evening meal. Chops, potato and broccoli. Ed helped himself to water from the decanter and spilled some on the tablecloth.

His father exploded, screaming and banging his fist on the table, making the plates jump. 'You stupid bugger,' he roared. 'Can't you get anything right! It's one thing after another with you.'

'But Peter,' his mother said gently, 'Ed didn't mean it. A little water, nothing else. It was an accident.'

Recalling that moment in years to come, Ed realised that it would have been wiser for his mother to say nothing. Any defence when rage has reached its insane height, is seen as provocation, red rag to a bull.

'And there you go again,' his father was still shouting, a line of foam appearing at the corner of his mouth, 'always defending him, as if he can do no wrong, and as for you…if it hadn't have been for you, if you had…' He stood suddenly, knocking his chair backwards to the floor with a bang, and marched from the room.

It hadn't occurred to Ed until then. He was at fault. He'd never thought otherwise – he had been disobedient – but his father was also blaming his mother. His father saw them as complicit. He'd tried to apologise to them for not looking after Todd. Of course he had. Several times. Stumbled apologies that were halted with a raised hand as if an apology might demand a reasonable response. Even a forgiving response. But he more than ever felt the need to go to his mother and convince her that she was blameless, that what she'd asked of him on that terrible day was completely reasonable.

She was defending him, aware of his pain and guilt while nursing her own. He started to wish that she'd shout at him. Outrage served a purpose for those giving vent to it. It could shift blame, even nourish a person's sense of their own righteousness.

He went to her in the days that followed the dinner table episode, and owned the blame yet again, but she refused to become angry. They rarely spoke about it but when they did, she conceded that he'd been disobedient, but insisted that it wasn't his fault.

A fortnight later, his father left without warning in the early hours of the morning. Half his clothes still hung in the wardrobe. Nothing else was taken. Neither of them saw him again. Gone was the man with the weekend chocolate surprises, and the good-natured singing out of tune. The image of the silver-haired back of his neck as he drove the old Ford Prefect that aroused incipient feelings of human fallibility and its ally, love, lingered, at least for a while. He never wrote, and didn't leave an address where he could be contacted.

Ed and his mother lived together for close to a decade, struggling to make ends meet. She worked for a few years before retiring, or being retired, with a small pension. Ed worked on a paper run, and dropping advertising pamphlets in people's letter boxes until he was old enough for more adult work after school and on weekends.

Ever since 'the accident', as she referred to it, his mother had changed. She was a good mother, at least in the early years of their life as a couple, but she became quieter and had retreated into herself. She was affectionate to Ed sporadically, sometimes ignoring him, and sometimes swamping him, holding and not letting him go as if her life depended on it. Always silent.

After a few years, her behaviour became more erratic. She'd forget to cook the evening meal, and Ed would discover that there was no food in the house and would have to ride his bike to the supermarket.

Sometimes the house was immaculate, and at other times a mess. She'd stop in the middle of something and forget what she was doing, or sit in the same place for hours staring out a window. He found her once at dusk in the nearby park. She said she wasn't sure how to get home, and besides, the trees kept whispering to her. It was this erratic behaviour that must have prompted her early retirement, no doubt enforced or at least encouraged by employers.

By his early to mid-secondary school years, he had virtually become her single carer, grasping at her rare lucid moments when she'd talk to him like his mother of old, and shower him with affection. These bright spots in their relationship became rarer and more short-lived.

It became increasingly difficult for him to study for his Higher School Certificate because of his mother's needs, her accidents, bizarre interruptions and the constant surprises. On the day of his first HSC English exam, she needed his help, and he arrived at the school a few minutes after the exam had begun.

His social life was almost non-existent, as he made so many excuses to his school friends, they stopped asking him out. He was attracted to a few girls over these years, and they to him, and while a couple of them saw his plight, were sympathetic and willing to help, the demands of a steady relationship were impossible, and the girls drifted away to find less harried partners.

By the time he finished school, doing better than he expected, his mother had deteriorated, and her care was taken out of his hands. His protests to the intervening authorities were half-hearted. His need to look after her was tempered by the realisation that she would be better looked-after elsewhere. And as some of the neighbours pointed out, if things got worse, there were some things it wasn't appropriate for a boy to be doing for his mother. Besides, he was exhausted.

Even so, the day his mother was taken to the institution entrusted with her care was the most painful day he'd ever experienced. Her walk from the cab was slow but purposeful. She went without a murmur, uncomplaining as she always had been.

As they entered the large double doors, held open for them by an attractive young nurse, he carrying all her possessions in one large suit-case, his mother took his arm, squeezed it, and looked intently at him with her weak, milky blue eyes. He could have sworn it was love that shone from them.

He felt he'd betrayed her.

3

If Ed's memories suddenly ignited and were quickly extinguished, sometimes forever, Lucy's were more lasting. She was born in Newcastle, the nearest city hospital to the family farm at Murrurundi, a sprawling huddle of communal life in the Hunter Valley.

The family lived in a large house on acres that after they'd left, became prime real estate and a celebrated horse stud. Lucy had a sister and two older brothers. She remembered the broad sweeping veranda around the house, and the trek to the free-standing outside toilet.

She had several other entrenched memories. The drought and the struggle for her father to keep the farm running. The time she saw her father puncture the stomach of a dead cow to allow the gas to escape before burning it. The trips to town in the old utility. And her infants' school education at the small local Catholic school, and her variable treatment by the nuns, the time she was smacked around the legs for fetching a reader that was at a more sophisticated level than that prescribed for children of her age.

When she was seven, the family moved to Sydney and lived in the eastern suburbs among wealthy relatives whose sense of entitlement was to become a pervasive influence in her maturing years. She despised the conceit that came with entitlement, and her relatives' subtle way of asserting their superiority over her own battling family.

She attended Loreto Kirribilli, where the girls were the children of wealthy parents. She was well-liked, though aware of the difference in privilege, and was invited to all the girls' birthday parties, where expensive gifts were often exchanged. Her mother struggled to provide a modest gift for such occasions, and, unlike most of the girls, Lucy wore her only party dress for each of the birthday parties. This contrast informed her adult need to be elegantly and well presented at all times, and gave her a keen appreciation of the less fortunate.

She performed well in her final school exams, completed a one-year secretarial course, and was employed by a branch of the public service. The work was repetitive and dull, and she found herself longing for more of a challenge. More of what, though? It may have been a sense of freedom that she craved, an autonomy that was denied her by the constraints of a formal, all-girls education. Travel became a wished-for priority.

Her need to 'break loose' was as much a reflection of her own naivete, that she grudgingly acknowledged, as a powerful awakening of her attractiveness to men. She'd had a few dates in her school years with different boys, all acne and embarrassment, but with no one who earned the status of boyfriend.

Slightly plump in her mid-school years, she graduated with a slim and shapely figure, deep brown eyes, full blonde hair to her waist, and a face that shone with openness and a willingness to engage.

Entering the workforce, she was pleased with how she'd evolved as an adult, with her appearance that she spent time cultivating, and with her sexual awareness that was newly emerging, opening like a springtime flower.

In her first year at work, she went on many dates, none of them serious. There was no readiness to commit, so dating was a smorgasbord of casual encounters. She saw this phase of her life as a playground for the growth of maturity, a time of simple pleasures before they morphed into an idyllic or harsh reality. Premature commitment or intimacy were not yet part of her story's script.

Some of her old school girlfriends who were struggling to maintain serious relationships were critical, condemning her as a social/sexual butterfly, but Lucy was not 'a tease', she was an enquirer, an explorer, testing inter-gender conventions and how they operated. She was never indifferent to the feelings of others, and took a genuine interest in them. She was alarmed and upset when one of her dates cried, saying he wanted to see a lot more of her. She was puzzled by feeling jealous when a work colleague, one she did not find very appealing, chose another girl to date, and not herself.

That all changed when she met Daniel.

*

Daniel Westerly was born at Northmead, a middle-class suburb to the north of Sydney where he attended local state schools. An only child, he didn't fit a common belief that such children are spoilt. Yet while he was reared to share his possessions and accept responsibility for his actions, he did develop a fierce determination to get what he wanted, probably legacy of humble beginnings.

This single-mindedness need not be seen as a criticism unless it challenges the dignity of people. It didn't involve riding roughshod over others. He kept a certain sensitivity to their needs, and pursued his wants with more of a cotton-wool diplomacy than aggression.

At times when he didn't get his own way in his growing years, his frustration would become hostility. But as he matured, he learned to accept these pitfalls as inevitabilities that life sometimes imposed.

A few days after his graduation from university where he studied business administration, he met Lucy. Who can explain the chemistry between people? The use of boxes to tick, criteria to test compatibility, are usually applied post facto when the relationship has grown, and as a lame way of proving the wisdom of mate selection…or as a reason for departure.

Their relationship grew, though they both laughed about their obvious differences, the boxes not ticked, moving within a week from frisson to love, to intimacy and a loose commitment.

A fortnight after graduation, and after the celebrations with family and peers for his second place in his course had wound down, he received a letter offering him a position at Macquarie Bank, possibly the most prestigious financial institution in Australia.

He was delighted. But there was a catch. It was in Melbourne. 'This is huge,' he excitedly told Lucy. He felt as if he'd won the lottery. 'You will come with me?' he asked more tentatively.

'But my work is here, Daniel,' she answered, biting her lip. 'And Mum and Dad…' She loved him, but their relationship was less than a fortnight old. She was torn, but reason told her it was premature to be making such a commitment. She did consider the possibility of joining him some time in the future, but she didn't say so.

'I do love you, Daniel,' she said, but he wasn't sure whether it was reassurance or a plea for him to stay.

Her resistance was palpable. He was miserable, lovelorn. He'd never felt this way about anyone before, but the offer from Macquarie Bank was a once in a lifetime opportunity.

In the few days before he had to reply to the offer, they spoke about the dilemma. Or rather, he did. Lucy was more silent. She was not ready to go, and not able to commit to a distant relationship.

Love won. He rejected the Macquarie Bank offer.

*

She was coming home. The crew on the red-eye special from Heathrow to Sydney were opening the window blinds, and even though it was early morning and an hour from Sydney, the fluffy clouds were dazzling white with sun. The light filled the plane as one shade after another was opened. It woke several passengers who drowsily moved their makeshift pillows, looked towards the toilets to see if a green light indicated a vacancy, or stood to find some morning essential from the overhead lockers. Others, who had scarcely slept at all, kept glazed eyes glued to the television screens in front of them. A few slept on oblivious.

'Not long now,' the woman sitting beside her said. 'Really looking forward to a hot shower. Can't wait.'

Lucy nodded. 'Yes, that'd be top of my list too.'

'Well, not the very top of mine,' the woman replied. 'Simon's top. I've really missed him. It's been ten days. He'll be waiting at the terminal, so I'd better go and spruce myself up.'

They'd had sporadic conversation throughout the flight, the pleasantries assumed on boarding and just as suddenly relinquished with landing.

'Is someone special waiting for you?' she asked, but not taking much notice.

'Yes,' Lucy answered, but showed no inclination to elaborate. The woman was too self-absorbed to inquire further.

Lucy and Daniel had become engaged before she left for overseas. In later years she'd wonder why. He was there when her close friend was killed in a road accident, and his constant presence and anticipation of her smallest needs was seductive. And while she battled to cope with her grief, he was seductive in the more literal sense.

Shortly after, the intuitive bond they'd felt as lovers crumbled as she returned to the desolation that had first attracted her to him. Her hope for a future with him was too much of an ideal to be sustained, too precarious, too prone to injured feelings. She resented their sexual intimacy, claiming he had taken her at a time of weakness. Why had she relented? He'd later quote Jung who spoke of the uncontrollability of real things, whatever that meant. But their separation became painful, and they reunited.

Engagement seemed the natural thing to do. They'd shared emotion. They'd shared their bodies. Perhaps this was what Jung meant by uncontrollability.

Daniel had no doubts. He was totally committed, even conforming to the conventional practice of proposing on one knee with the ring proffered in both hands. 'I can't tell you how happy you've made me,' he said, visibly shaken. 'I feel my life is finally complete.'

When her travelling companion had gone to the toilets, Lucy took a pile of letters from her hand luggage, annotations of a tender yet recently troubled past, giving them their sentient freedom from the rubber band that balled them together. She riffled through them, finding an early one. 'My darling Lucy,' it began.

Yesterday as I was communing with the natural world – nowhere better than walking on our beach – I stumbled across a couple lying in the sand, concealed by a dune and the approaching dusk. They were moving in synchrony if you know what I mean, their performance only dimly visible by a watery apricot, and their accompaniment the pounding surf.

They were oblivious to me as I passed, but I could see a woman's thigh snake-like curling around her lover, lit by a creamy Easter moon.

Of course I thought of you, of us, and felt a painful longing, all alone beneath the dozing stars. It's only been a fraction of the time you'll be away, and I wonder how I'll be able to endure the hours, weeks and months ahead. Did I say minutes?

Please write soon, and tell me you feel the same.

Daniel had pretensions to be a writer. The letter was typical of his prose when he'd strive for effect and often overwrite. Lucy wondered how long he'd spent writing it, and whether it was meant to impress as poetry. She read a second letter, one of many, written only ten days ago.

Dearest Lucy,

At last! Four months has been an eternity! I can't tell you how relieved I am that it's coming to an end. I know you don't want me to dwell on the anguish it's been, but I do hope you might have felt a little of the same. Kaiser misses you too. He's been a good boy, chasing Mrs Hislop's cat away, and crossing the days off on our doggie calendar.

I know you'll wait till I see you to talk about 'serious' things, about us, but can you give me an indication, a hint of what you're feeling? Nights when I go to bed, are fertile times for memories, pleasant and nightmarish. But I think of you when I'm having breakfast, going to work, mowing the lawn. I think you get the idea. I savour the good memories like one of those Ferrero Rocher chocolates you love.

You'd be proud of me. I've let nothing slip. Some rooms are freshly painted, the side fence has been replaced, and the lawns mown and the gardens weeded.

You have all my love, Luce. Looking forward to holding you again. So is Kaiser.

Your worshipping soulmate, D.

The woman returned from the toilet smelling of cheap perfume, and began filling in documents for customs.

Lucy returned the letter to her bag. At least he hadn't signed it 'husband-to-be'. He always liked to woo her with words, spoken and written. Whenever she became emotional, he'd tame what he called her rambling with a string of sober words.

'A trial separation,' she'd called it. That's the name it was always given. She remembered Daniel's face when she told him. He was crushed.

'Is there no other way?' he managed to say after a minute's tearful silence, the sitting room in his unit palpable with pain.

'Four months,' she'd said. 'I really need the time, Daniel,' she continued gently, mindful of his hurt. 'There's a great deal I have to think about. I can't do it here, and I can't do it overnight.' It seemed a well-reasoned excuse, but if she'd been completely honest, she'd have admitted that the separation caused her no real heartache. She wanted to get away. She needed to get away.

It wasn't negotiable. She'd already arranged to live for four months with her sister in Tunbridge Wells. She'd even arranged some part-time work. She'd been looking forward to a change of scene, wondering if it would also mean a change of heart. It was also an adventure, an escape to freedom, beyond her stuffy world. She'd given notice at work, and planned to see as much of England and Wales as possible.

She was gone a few days later, insisting that she alone catch a taxi to the airport, and leaving a mournful Daniel and Kaiser together in his sitting room. Kaiser belonged to them both, bought as a rescue dog after their engagement. He lived with Daniel.

'A trial separation,' he reflected, as he heard the taxi depart on the gravel driveway. The idea of a trial implied undergoing a test, answering to some sort of accountability. It seemed to him that the only protagonists in such a trial were time and circumstance. And they were fickle allies.

The crew was given landing instructions by the captain, and the plane began its slow descent. Behind that last letter was her rough copy of the one she'd sent in reply. She wouldn't normally make a copy but it was important to convey the right message, and not to mislead.

Dear Daniel,

I'd really like to stay here in Tunbridge Wells longer. I've had an enjoyable time, working and sight-seeing. England is a wonderful place, and I'd like to see more of it. So much history. Elaine has made my stay very comfortable.

But I did say four months, and it wouldn't be fair on you to prolong my stay, so I'll be leaving on the twelfth on the red-eye special.

I cannot really tell you how things are between us. I was hoping that being away, and in a distant place, might help me to clarify things, but that hasn't been the case. Perhaps when I see you again, everything will become clearer.

I have wondered how you've been coping, and Kaiser of course. I hope you've been cooking yourselves decent meals.

I'd rather you didn't pick me up at the airport. I'll let you know when I'm back. Keep well.

Lucy.

Lucy found it difficult to analyse why she was so uncertain about Daniel. They were different. He was idealistic, certainly romantic. Possibly unrealistic. She knew he saw her as practical, pragmatic, probably unromantic. But surely everyone could be a romantic if the right person inspired them to be. But what point was there in cataloguing differences. Did they have anything to do with finding happiness together.

She recalled how terrible it had been when she told him she didn't think things were working between them. It seemed to have come as a surprise for him.

'What can I do?' he'd asked plaintively like a child who wants nothing more than to please.

He looked so forlorn she thought of telling him to forget what she'd just said. Instead, she'd replied that what makes people unhappy, or what causes a breakdown between people can't always be changed by actions. It's often simply who they are, a matter of sense, feeling, chemistry.

*

She insisted on taking a taxi to the airport. Didn't want any fraught goodbyes. She sat in the departure lounge feeling half-real, questioning what she was doing. But the thought of her travels uplifted her. The world was full of exciting possibilities.

She watched the threads of cloud floating across a sky struggling for colour, observed the landing planes mope home like scolded dogs with noses to the scent. Waiting passengers dozed, and others read. Families chatted till, cliché-spent, their thoughts attenuated to fairy breath.

Her flight number was eventually called for boarding. For Lucy, the world was mutating to endless uncertainties, but she wasn't fazed. She couldn't wait to experience them.

It wasn't a comfortable trip, but her sister did all she could to restore her spirits, and make her feel part of the family's life. She organised a job in the university library, to give her purpose and security. Lucy ran each morning, bought a leotard and went to pilates classes once a week, collected her sister's young children from school on the odd occasion, and shared the cooking responsibilities. It didn't take long to 'settle in'.

She'd only been there for four days when the first of many letters arrived. It must have been written the day she left.

My dear Lucy,

Forgive me, but the urge to write was just too great. I know you didn't want to hear from me so soon, and that you needed your space. Perhaps I'm being selfish but my way is to talk it all through, whatever 'it all' is, rather than walk away and hope that it will get clearer by some process of osmosis.

It may seem ridiculous to say I'm missing you when it's only been two hours since you left, but that's probably when it's the most painful, with the realisation that you have actually gone, and that it will be months before I see you again. Will it become any easier? Will I be able to adapt to your absence? I don't think so.

I don't want to pressure you, Luce, but if you could tell me how I could change, even if it's only a couple of things I can do to improve, to work on while you're away. I can't make any promises, but I'll do everything I can.

I hope you had a comfortable trip. [The next sentence was heavily crossed out. One could only surmise why.] Say hello to Elaine from me. Kaiser sends his love.

You're my life Luce, D xx.

Lucy was not pleased to receive the letter. Not so soon. But she knew Daniel was hurting, and through no real fault of his own. And she did have responsibilities towards him, even if she had made it clear that she needed her space. So she waited for a week and wrote back, a restrained letter thanking him for his letter, and telling him she was having valuable reflection time, and that it wasn't as simple as listing the things he could do to change. It ended with an appeal for patience.

Time dragged for Daniel, a procession of near endless days to face an achromatic world, to force himself to leave the bed and room that had grown with them, to hear the dawn's mournful lament of the crows with their human sounding call, and to brave their friends' innocent 'where's Lucy' questions.

*

Kaiser was there to meet her when she let herself into Daniel's unit, at first with a growl, until recognition dawned and he leapt on her, furiously wagging his tail. Daniel was at work, not expecting her till later.

She unpacked and, as she'd missed breakfast on the plane, made herself a salad. Daniel must have bought groceries in anticipation. It was still late morning and she decided to go on a run.

Unlike the busy streets of Tunbridge Wells where runners had to dodge cars and pedestrians, and wait at crossings, the roads near Daniel's unit were not major thoroughfares, and wound through bush that at different times of the year was in full bloom. She'd missed her runs here.

She'd been running for several minutes, filling her lungs with the scented air, and enjoying the birdsong, when she saw something ahead in the ditch at the side of the road. At first she thought it was rubbish or a discarded overcoat, but as she approached, she could see that it was a man lying still.

He wasn't old. About her own age, dressed in professional-looking navy running garb, lying helplessly on his back, making no effort to move, and in obvious pain. He lay in the hollow of baked clay watching her come.

Lucy sprinted to his side, saw him clutching at his chest, and instantly phoned 000 on her mobile that she took everywhere in case urgent messages were needed.

She made him comfortable as best she could, sitting in the hollow at the side of the road and resting his head on her lap, stroking his damp forehead, watching his startled eyes watching hers, questioning, imploring help. She held him like a child.

She'd later try to remember what she said to him. Probably the soothing things you might say to an injured child: 'You're going to be fine', 'Try to remain calm', 'The ambulance is on its way.' She'd try to remember what force passed between them, or more particularly what passed from her.

He tried to speak but couldn't, and she'd always wondered what his dying words might have been. In a hardened ochre hollow with the singing of birds, and a profusion of sunlit yellow pellets of wattle agitating against a royal blue sky, she sensed acceptance birthing in his eyes, and felt the dying flutter. She felt she died a little too.

It was only a minute before the ambulance arrived, but nothing could be done. After the ambulance men's confirming check, and the telltale shaking of heads, they showed more concern about her than the man for whom there was no need for any further intervention. She later learned his name was William.

'Can we drive you home, miss?' they asked with obvious concern, but Lucy declined despite their protests that she'd received a shock.

The ambulance left, and she continued sitting in the hollow for what must have been hours, sometimes clasping both drawn-up knees, sometimes lying prostrate against the warm clay, feeling its honest and epicene embrace.

She imagined Daniel, probably at home now, being delighted by her early return. Perhaps being encouraged by it. He'd kiss her, gently, careful not to force anything, showing his pleasure at seeing her again, mix her a brandy and dry, her favourite drink, as she, a distant look in her eyes prepared to say a final goodbye. Four months had changed nothing. A few seconds did.

She told him straight out. Better that way, far better than exchanging the usual pleasantries, waiting for the other to make a move, playing verbal games, clumsily evading the customary hug. She could have told him about Tunbridge Wells, her part-time job, and living with Elaine. She could have asked him about the meals he'd cooked while she was away, and enquired about Kaiser. She didn't.

'Did you get my letters?' he asked, looking stricken. It was a pointless question unless she knew how many he'd sent, but he needed time to think or know how to react.

Lucy felt his pain overwhelm her. She was scared.

After half a minute of excruciating silence, he wanted to know how long she'd known about her decision. His lips were pursed and the fury was stamped on his face. His arms hung by his side. His fists were clenched.

'Only when I got back,' she whispered, her resolve failing. How could she explain how a stranger dying in her arms had been the catalyst. She couldn't explain it herself.

'There's nothing then…' The last residue of hope.

Lucy shook her head. She was trying not to cry. It would weaken her stance, make her vulnerable to his pleadings, like an animal sensing the fear in its prey. She knew she had hurt him terribly, led him on for all these months, and then discarded him. She hadn't meant to.

Daniel knew it was over. Knew there was no hope. Didn't believe her that the decision had only just become clear to her. Reckoned she never had any intention of returning to him. The time for pleading had long passed. She had reduced him to begging, futile begging, and he hated her for the indignity of it.

'I will never, never as long as I live…' he began, slowly enunciating each word, and looking at her, fit to kill.

'I'm so sorry, Daniel, so sorry,' she whispered, retreating like a cowering animal, conscious of every backward step.

4

'Any luck spreading the net, Kane?'

'No. Only a few in the neighbouring street knew her well. One of them, a close friend, said she'd had a long relationship not long ago that finished badly. The fella was really bitter, so probably said some threatening things to her.'

'We can't just assume that. He got a name?'

'Yes, Westerly. Doing a few checks. Tell you when I've got more.'

'Good work, Kane. You're learning fast.'

Kane Roberts was the young officer who first addressed Ed on the night of the murder. His task had been to keep people away from the crime scene. Policing hadn't been his first choice for a career, but the training had kindled his enthusiasm. It was his first year out of the academy and he lived with his girlfriend Sarah, a teacher of domestic science at the local high school. She was protective of him, believing he didn't have the 'steel' to be effective as a policeman. He was going to prove her wrong.

'Anyone else of interest, Ken?'

'A single source said she was seen around the town with an Adrian Passmore, a lawyer, coffee once or twice, that sort of thing. I spoke to Passmore…helping her with legal matters on her father's estate. He was surprised when I asked him about the coffee dates. That's news to me, he said. Her other siblings are wasted spaces. Left it all to her. He was shocked when he heard the news, really upset. And the source was hardly reliable, an anonymous phone call. I think we can rule him out.'

Ken Carpenter lived alone, and had a deep respect for his superior. He had, after all, followed him from Tamworth after his messy divorce, and envied Clive his happy marriage with Elizabeth. But envy didn't mean bitterness. He was meticulous in his pursuit of crime, scorning lack of order in police work, believing it was on a continuum with disrespect for the laws of the land and ordered home life.

'I suppose we need that sort of help, but ninety-nine per cent of the time it's hearsay or scandal-mongering.' Clive shared Ken's belief in being thorough.

'There's another small thing. Duggan at the Chatswood station said a man, the boss of the printing company she worked for, came in, very shaken, said it was probably nothing, but there'd been a work dispute involving Lucy….the other woman was fired over it, and was very bitter…screaming blue murder.'

'Screaming at who?'

'Both Lucy and him.'

'Better follow it up with Duggan. Early days, but any thoughts, Kane?' Clive wanted his young probationary officer to feel included.

'Well, Clive, I don't think it could have been a burglary gone wrong. None of the doors or windows were forced. And there was no sign of a struggle. It must have been someone she knew. Of course it's always possible that the door was unlatched and the killer just walked in.'

'My thoughts exactly. I still think it was someone she knew. Keep digging. It'll all unravel. Always does. Just think, fellas, both of you will be running the show in a few years, and I'll be fishing, going back to Elizabeth or one of the girls for fried fish and tartare.'

*

It wasn't while walking the dog, bumping into each other at the supermarket or library, or at the conventional potpourri of expectant men and women partygoers longing for romantic diversions. They met standing in line outside the polling booth at the local school waiting to vote at the federal election. He dropped his how to vote sheet, and it fluttered to the ground behind him. She stooped in the moving queue to pick it up.

'Thank you,' he said.

'I can see you're a Labor supporter,' she commented with a smile.

'Yes…I'm Ed.'

'Whose head?'

'No…my name…is Ed.'

They both started to giggle, and she reached out her hand by way of introduction.

'I'm Lucy.'

'Whosie?'

'Touché,' and they started to laugh.

Other people near them in the line were grinning.

All nonsense, but she needed to laugh, and her laughter belied her fragility. She'd returned from overseas three weeks ago, and was still feeling guilty. She'd hurt Daniel. She should have told him of her serious doubts, but she'd been hopeful that all might be well between them. Feelings could be capricious. She might have been expecting too much. If it hadn't been for the dying runner she'd come across, and the crystallising effect it had, who knows what she'd have done.

She should have insisted he take the job of a lifetime in Melbourne. Had Daniel been right in his last words? Did she always know it would end like this? Perhaps she had betrayed him, and in doing so she'd hurt herself. She wasn't feeling right with the world.

They had coffee together at a local café after voting, 'Whosie' and 'Head', and enjoyed each other's company. The attraction was obvious. This was the beginning of their relationship. They laughed a lot over that first coffee, inventing the nonsense language that sometimes has its beginnings when comedy is part of an attraction.

The igniting of a relationship is often a matter of timing. People aren't static. A month earlier or later in the evolving history of one or both partners may fail to produce the spark. The timing for Ed and Lucy was right. Serendipity. They needed the chemistry their different forces created.

They started to date and the flame didn't die. Lucy often initiated, her spirit of adventure and organisation asserting itself. Ed wasn't as self-assured as Daniel had been, and was more introspective. He'd had less experience of the world than Lucy, though his little experience had been a baptism by fire. Lucy sometimes thought him too yielding to the wishes of others, too acquiescent.

He did take the lead for their first weekend away somewhere across the water from Palm Beach. It was three months after their first meeting, and he was excited, confirming and reconfirming the details. It was the beginning of something very new.

After checking in to the old guest house shortly after lunch, accommodation that the web described as 'old-fashioned, tired yet comfortable', they enjoyed the home-cooked afternoon tea of scones with jam and clotted cream that Mrs Willoughby provided, and went for a long walk on a beach, admiring the driftwood that had been washed ashore, and listening to the symphony of bird sounds and lapping water.

They returned to a still-water inlet not far from the guest house where they sat touching shoulders on an old fallen tree trunk.

It was soon dusk, and the sparkle from a low rising moon tapered towards them across a dozing ocean. They stood looking across the water. A few yachts slumbered in the bay. Neither gave voice to what was growing between them. It was hard to articulate what they'd never experienced before, a feeling that shut out everything beyond them. The sky was a soft tangerine, immensely beautiful.

'Magnificent,' he said aloud. 'It's beyond description.'

'Try,' she said.

'I sometimes think that even trying to describe something as wonderful as this is like using it…the colours fade and it loses definition. It's probably better not to say any more.'

'Does that apply to describing feelings too?'

He wasn't sure if she was being provocative, but her face gave no clue.

'Perhaps it does,' he said thoughtfully. 'Sometimes the feelings are so intense…'

He said no more but knelt on the hard apron of sand near the edge of quiet lapping water, and began to write a message with his finger, the gouged letters bold in the damp sand, the subject 'I', self-conscious now in her presence, and tethered to an 'l', hurrying to a generous 'o', the symbol of her sex, to 'v' that plunged to a hesitant cusp before his finger's quick ascent and glide to 'e'.

He stood, serious, his knees crumbed with sand, moved a few paces away, and inscribed 'you', the other side of love beyond himself.

Lucy, who'd been reading the message as it was written, smiled, kissed him on the cheek as he stood, and knelt, gesturing with her hand as a signal that she was about to reply with her own message. But as she began to write, the word 'and', they felt a few gobs of rain. The gentle tangerine sky had been overthrown by a cloak of slate grey, and darkness came sprinting across the sky, an enemy ambush. A wind started to howl, and it began to pour, obliterating his sand message.

Lucy swung round looking in all directions as if there might be safe haven out to sea before she started to run. The guest house was a few hundred metres away, and there were no caves, or shop awnings to protect them. No houses with a front veranda. Water was already swirling in the gutters, and puddles they couldn't dodge were splashing them as they ran.

Ed was the faster of the two, and kept turning, reaching out to her as if taking her hand would speed her progress. His gallantry was no help at all, but it was something he had to do.

They reached the guest house door sopping wet, and Ed couldn't help laughing. It may have been that he saw something comic in what had happened, or it may have been a bizarre defence against a more dreaded concern that their first time away may have been spoiled. He looked at her to determine if the latter was true. She was standing with her lank hair dripping onto her face, and her clothes pasted to her body, with the doggy smell of sodden wool.

She returned his look, feigning the distress of a small child about to cry, before she started to laugh. 'I'll have to wash my hair,' she said with the same pouting face and infant's voice.

'I thought we'd just done that,' he quipped, at ease now, and was given a gentle thump on the shoulder.

They made their way to their room, mindful of the water that was wetting the carpet.

'The soup of the day is minestrone,' he read from the menu in their room. 'That might be a good starter. That with hot buttered toast.'

Lucy was busy removing her sodden slacks.

'We're so lucky,' Ed said abstractedly.

'Yes, we are,' Lucy replied, and pulled him to her.

They stood like that, silent in a drenched embrace for fully a minute, cheek to wet cheek.

'Well, I did my best to rescue a damsel in distress,' he teased.

'And who was in distress?' she rallied. 'You were running around out there like a chook without its head.'

'Bathtime for you,' he ordered, 'before you soak Mrs Willoughby's carpet,' and with her stockinged feet standing on top of his, and her arms still around his neck, he walked her laughing to the old chipped enamel bath that stood on clawed feet as if it was going to walk out the door. 'Leave the water in for me when you've finished,' and he turned on the groaning tap with instantly steaming water.

She emerged twenty minutes later, wrapped in a fluffy towel, rosy from the heat, sweet-smelling and somehow softer-looking than before, no longer bared and hardened by the reduction of rain.

'My turn,' he said softly, the dizzying feeling of standing on the apron of beach an hour ago returning. The same feeling, but different. How? Less rarefied, more personal, more substantial and real?

She stood still just beyond the bathroom door, looking at him in a curious way, her head slightly tilted. There was a message in her eyes he tried to read. He thought better of asking. It was better left unsaid. Yes, some things were beyond description.

Was it the heat from the bath, a creeping realisation, the crack in carapace's reserve, the storm a harbinger of rites of passage they would soon share in the lumpy double bed with words that would tumble hot and wet? This was no fantasy, he'd later tell himself. Some may well create the beauty of a waterfall from a lifeless stream, but this image would remain the same, inviolate.

*

The marriage was a happy one. Lucy had no doubts as she had with Daniel. Her attraction to Ed was more than circumstantial. It was gravitational. It had surprised her, even though she'd had no image of the man she might end up with.

There are always tensions when two people are committed to a close mutuality of living, but these were not major and were easily resolved. Disagreements were not allowed to fester and lead to silence, resentment, and end in dislocation.

Lucy was the extrovert, both because it was her nature, and because her friends expected her to assume that role. Ed was more of an introvert, but would often surprise by sometimes being the life of the party when he was more typically its remote commentator.

After six months of marriage, they moved from a rented unit into a three-bedroom Cape Cod house in Turramurra. They were helped by the sale of his family home, to which his mother would not return. It had a large veranda, a priority of Lucy's, and a sentimental reminder of her Murrurundi days. A study for them both to share, a modern kitchen and a large yard. There were the usual jokes about how the two extra bedrooms might be filled.

'Oliver or Olivia in this one,' Ed would say. 'Which is it to be?'

'Sure, Ed,' Lucy would reply, 'but not for a little while yet.'

They made friends quickly, entertaining neighbours soon after moving in, and taking an interest in their children. Lucy was delighted to see how good Ed was with the little ones. The neighbours returned the favour.

One of these occasions was significant for them both. A test of sorts. It was a Christmas drinks party and virtually everyone in the street was invited. Loud music, noise to match, frenzied dancing and alcohol on tap.

In one of his less extroverted moods, Ed escaped to the balcony, grateful for the silence, and was looking at the houses basking below when he was approached by Trish Stead, on the pretext of having a cigarette. She was a brassy blonde in her late thirties, with a heavily made-up face that didn't quite disguise the early signs of ageing. She wore a silver lame dress that hugged, or held her ample curves in feminine order.

'Not your scene, is it, Ed?' she said, greeting him like a fellow sufferer, and raising her chin to blow smoke into the air.

'No, not really,' Ed answered, tempted to fan away the smoke. 'I prefer small groups, say six or eight, where you have the opportunity to have a conversation. Of course there's a place for this too,' he felt the need to add.

'Do you find this,' and she gestured dismissively towards the room full of guests, 'intimidating?'

'Not intimidating, no,' he answered. 'A bit false sometimes, I suppose. And the bigger the group, the more artificial it becomes.'

'You're an interesting man, Ed,' she said, stubbing her cigarette on the balcony edge by leaning forward, revealing a deep cleavage with jouncing breasts, and crossing her solarium glossy legs that hitched her dress well up her thighs. 'Tell me what you mean by false.'

'Not natural. Everyone's trying to impress. There's no opportunity for talk. I'm sure most of these people are nice, but it's a situation where they probably feel they can't be themselves….have to be larger than life.'

'I feel exactly the same, Ed,' Trish emoted, and placed her hand on his arm. 'Small groups for me too. A foursome is perfect. Four people who really care for each other, who can talk to each other, and who are willing to share, to share whatever.' She recrossed her legs, leaning towards him, exposing more of her thighs. 'Your wife and Gordon seem to be getting on like a house on fire.' She smiled, and gestured again to the room, where Ed could just make out Lucy in deep conversation with Gordon Stead.

Ed was uncomfortable. He knew where this conversation was heading. Her beringed hand was still resting on his arm. It had to be deliberate. Her long, artificial blood-red nails morphed into talons.

'Perhaps I'd better rescue her.' Ed thought he'd found a means of escape. 'It's been pleasant talking to you, Trish,' he said, stood, and headed inside, leaving Trish looking stony-faced, and reaching for another cigarette.

Meanwhile, Gordon Stead was proving to be less subtle than his wife, if that were possible.

'You're an attractive woman, Lucy,' he told her. 'Clever too, from what I hear.'

'Why thank you, Gordon,' Lucy replied, but refused to return the compliment. She found him seedy and unattractive. 'I'm sure Trish is more attractive than I am.'

Gordon failed to see the implied criticism. He thought Lucy was playing a cat-and-mouse game, and smiled, believing his chatting-up was going well. 'Two attractive women. Aren't I the lucky one?' This was schoolboy lack of subtlety. He was speaking as if Lucy was already another conquest, and she was becoming increasingly irritated. He was appraising her through roving steel grey eyes as though she were a piece of meat.

'Perhaps you and Ed would like to join us for dinner one night soon. I can see he's quite taken with Trish,' and he pointed to the balcony, where Lucy could see Trish leaning towards Ed. 'A small, intimate gathering, a nice meal, good wine, and who knows…'

'Care for a dance, Mrs Grainger?' Ed had made his escape and crashed Gordon's overture.

Gordon seemed put out by the interruption but quickly regained his composure as Ed whisked her away. 'Ed, I was just saying to your wife…' he hastened to say, but they were gone, and left the party as soon as they thought it appropriate.

'What a horrid man,' Lucy repeated, lying in bed that night. 'There was no doubt what he wanted. Yuk! The very thought of it.'

'Did I rescue you in time?' Ed answered to lighten her mood.

'You rescued me before I poured my glass of Shiraz over his head. I was just about to do so, and come and rescue you. His wife looked like she was about to devour you.' She paused for a second as if considering whether to continue. 'You didn't like her, did you, Ed?'

'Hell, no. She was awful.'

'Not just a wee bit sexy…big bust, long brown legs?' Lucy was relieved and had started to tease him.

'There's only one person I want,' Ed replied. 'Only one person I need.'

And Lucy, snuggling up to him, could tell he was serious.

5

'We found them going through a folder in his bedside table drawer.' Ken pulled them from his inside coat pocket. 'They weren't concealed, so we assume his wife knew all about them.'

'When was this?' Clive asked, moving his feet off the desk.

'Only yesterday. Ed hasn't returned there yet and he gave us permission to have a look around, take anything we need. It was Kane's idea,' and he looked across the room to where the young officer was sitting. 'He thought it might be useful. I agree, you can pick up on little things even if you don't find anything...get a feel about people's lives.'

'I thought we did a thorough search,' Clive asked with dawning interest.

'We looked in the bedside tables, but didn't think going through every file or envelope in there would shed any light on the murder,' Ken answered.

'How many letters?'

'Eleven,' Kane replied, 'but that doesn't include slips of paper, and notes written on paper serviettes from cafes. Doesn't look as if they were posted, and they're crumpled, folded over and stuck together, so if she didn't give them to him by hand, she must have put them in the letter box. Mrs Grainger must have wondered what it was all about.'

'Anything revealing?' Clive asked, still only half-interested.

'Could be,' Ken answered. 'We were a bit interested after the first letter, weren't we, Kane? We started to wonder about Ed Grainger. Is this, what do you call it – a grand amour – but as we read on, we realised that it was all one-sided, and this woman was a real weirdo.'

'Somehow, I don't think Ed is a womaniser,' Clive replied. 'I don't know why, but I kind of like the guy. OK, let's hear some of it.'

'Get ready.' Ken smiled as if a surprise was coming. He took the first letter from its envelope and began to read:

Dear Ed,

When you first spoke to me outside the shops, I felt something real special, and I'm sure that you felt like me too. It doesn't happen very often, does it, like when two people feel the same and make a connexion? So I asked in the cake shop there, about you I mean, and they says your name was Grainger, that you and your wife come in with an order for vanilla slices, and they spelled it for me, so I wrote this letter.

Vanilla slices are my favourite to, so it is something more we might have in common. Do you want to know more about me? I hope you do. I'm thirty and married to Derek, who works fixing bridges. You know what I look like, unless you wasn't looking. I hope you liked what you saw. I liked what I saw. I play tennis – do you? – go out with my friends, and I watch television. You'll have to guess my favourite show. Am I older than you? I think I might be, Ed, and does it matter?

Please write back to me and tell me about your wife. Is she real pretty? I bet she is, and hope she is for you, but not too pretty…

'I think that's enough,' Clive interrupted. 'I get the drift.'

'Signed "your ever-loving friend, Berice",' Kane added. 'Doesn't sound the sort of woman that Grainger would find attractive, but we thought the last bit about the wife could mean something.'

'And where do they go from there?' Clive asked.

'Listen,' Ken answered, 'this is the last one,' and he took the letter from the top of the pile. 'You might find this more revealing,' and he began to read, enjoying the attention.

Ed Grainger,

I'm not happy. No, I'm not happy at all. I have tried hard to be a good friend to you. I've suggested we meet and have a coffee and a vanilla slice, and even waited for you on one time but you didn't come. I've written I don't know how many letters and asked you to tell me about yourself and your very pretty wife but I haven't got any letters, not a single one.

I told Derek about you, and how we hit it off when we first met, and I now know that he is jealous. What do you think about that? Does it please you? Ed, you should treat a lady a lot, lot better because you are making me real mad!!

All right, I've had me/x/my winge and hope it doesn't make you feel so poor or guilty that you won't want to see me. I do love you, and that's another thing you have never told me and I wonder why not.

Ken stopped reading. 'Want me to go on?'

'No,' Clive replied, 'but you'd better leave the letters on my desk. I'm not sure what they can tell us, but I'd better go through them too. We should be thorough, so we'd better get Ed in for an interview about this Berice. Would you like to take the running on that, Ken? Oh, and Kane, how would you like to assist?'

'Do you want me to track down Berice?' Ken asked.

'Not just yet,' Clive answered. 'Let's see what Ed has to say first. And Ken, anything from this Berice since the murder?'

'Not that we know about.'

'All the more reason to talk to Ed.' Clive replaced his feet on the desk, deep in thought.

Ken hurried from the room to contact Ed. Kane was delighted to be included. He was liking Clive more and more.

*

While Berice Downing was proud of her independence, and indifferent to the status or power that others tried to exercise over her, she usually took her lead from Derek, her less intelligent and less couth husband.

There were few records of Derek's early life. He spent most of his childhood and youth in a travelling circus that visited small rural towns. His mother and father were probably circus entertainers who felt no responsibility for his rearing. He never knew them, so it is likely they moved on to another circus. His early work consisted of feeding and mucking out the cages of the animals, cueing the acts for the performances, and running errands. It's probable that he had no schooling, and only ever learned the rudiments of reading and writing from Flo, a dwarf, half of a comic act cruelly named 'One and a Half'. They lived together in a circus caravan, defending each other from insult and sharing their limited resources. 'She was my real mother,' he later told Berice. 'The only one I ever had.'

Despite often being hungry, he grew into a big man, and after several years away in an effort to make good on his own, he returned to the circus to double as a strong man, lifting two scantily dressed women hanging from each end of a staff, and as a clown. Many of the performers had to change costumes quickly or apply make-up and appear in another role.

During his time away, he worked at several jobs, either leaving or being fired for giving cheek and brawling. He was unschooled in how to manage his life, and his venture to go it alone failed.

As a young boy, he had to stand up for himself, and as an adult welcomed a good fight, deliberately provoking them. Any excuse was good enough. He once broke a man's nose for looking sideways at him at a pub counter. He spent a month in a local lock-up before returning to the relative safety of the circus.

Berice Downing (née Ferguson) was reared on a small isolated farm in the west of the state. Even as a toddler, she was given responsibility for feeding the animals and milking. She'd later talk to Derek about their shared fondness for animals.

It wasn't a happy childhood. Her parents were ill-educated and abusive, punishing her by locking her in a cupboard. Her fear of the dark and closed spaces remained with her into her adult years. Sometimes she was punished because she made a mess of the milking, particularly in the icy mornings, not having enough strength in her tiny hands to grasp the teats of the cows. She was never meek and mild, and her defiance was answered by a hard slap across the face and having to go without whatever little there was for a meal.

She loved her small two-teacher school, both because she did well at her lessons, and because it was a relief from life at home. It gave her world a sanity she hadn't known.

While many children wilt and become withdrawn in the face of abuse, the punishments Berice suffered steeled her willpower, making her passionate in pursuing her rights, refusing to bow down to authority she didn't respect, and sometimes crossing the line of acceptable behaviour.

The instability and abuse of her childhood may have been a factor in her unusual attachment to Ed, a not uncommon feature of obsession. She'd never behaved towards anyone as she'd behaved with Ed.

Marriage had been a chance to escape, and she did have to literally flee her parents' clutches. But the marriage was more than convenience. It was a union of like-minded souls. Berice and Derek were alter egos. For Berice, Derek was 'a man's man', never taking a backward step. For Derek, Berice was a real woman, nothing prissy about her, strong and practical, someone who knew her own mind.

*

It was at the cake shop they'd met. Ed was about to enter for the vanilla slices Lucy had requested for their afternoon tea visitors. Berice was coming out, both hands carrying bags of shopping, and Ed opened the door for her, stepping aside to let her pass.

'Very kind,' she said, and once outside made no move to go on her way, but stood watching him, half-blocking the entrance. There was a faint tremble in her mulberry-coloured lips.

'Everything all right?' Ed asked, looking at the pale and strained face topped with what looked like a forest of uncombable black hair.

She nodded before her barely audible 'yes'. She seemed to be overcome and he didn't understand why.

When Ed had been seventeen, he'd been introduced to a girl at a dance, a slim and delicate auburn-haired girl his own age, and had been instantly overwhelmed, literally weak in the knees, finding it difficult to be coherent in the few words they exchanged. Smitten. Surely he hadn't had the same impact on this parcelled woman. Or had he? Why else would she be standing there, fixed to the pavement.

'Well, I'd better get the cakes,' he said smiling, nodding towards the half-open fly-screen door, and as an afterthought, 'Nice to have met you.'

'Been really nice…' Her words trailed away as he entered the shop.

As he waited at the counter for his order of vanilla slices, he could see her outline through the fly-screen mesh, waiting outside, and feeling uncomfortable with her reaction, contrived conversation with the salesgirl until she seemed to have gone. It might have been some sort of medical episode.

'You have an admirer,' the salesgirl smiled, nodded to the door and winked.

The first letter arrived a day later, and his reaction was half-humorous and half-serious. Some of her comments about their meeting were so far from what he remembered, they were comical, but you couldn't be so easily dismissive of someone's affection. He was alarmed and showed the letter to Lucy, who felt the same as he did.

'Perhaps you should write a short reply, saying your wife is not just pretty. She is beautiful, and the centre of your world,' Lucy said light-heartedly.

But Ed had no intention of responding in any way.

Letters continued to arrive. The initial references to a 'connection' between them became 'love' in the third letter, and she wrote of her disappointment that he didn't profess his love for her. She had little doubt at first that he felt the same way, and condemned him for his reserve, 'not opening his heart' as she called it. Several of the early letters asked him to meet her at a particular café at a time she nominated. Ed didn't go.

He showed each of the letters to Lucy, and while the letters were at first dismissed as fantasy, they both became more concerned. A scorned woman might be dangerous, but what about one who was delusional as well? One who'd lost touch with what was real? Sometimes there was a note with a sentence or two on a torn and folded scrap of paper stuffed in the letter box.

They discussed what they might do. At first, Lucy had thought Ed should speak to Berice and attack her illusions, but as the letters continued to arrive, they questioned the woman's grip on reality, and dismissed the idea believing it would lead to more trouble. Lucy realised it was getting out of hand, and it might be time to call the police. It could spell danger.

Ed favoured doing nothing and waiting for her to lose interest. 'It's hardly a police matter,' he said, 'a woman telling a man how she feels about him.'

'It is if she keeps doing it, Ed,' Lucy answered. 'It is if the woman is obviously delusional. And what about the letters? It's harassment.'

After the first few letters, and his failure to turn up at the café she'd chosen, he saw her following him one day. She was stalking him. Her mop of black hair was unmistakable. She kept her distance, not realising that he'd seen her. At least he was grateful that she didn't accost him, if that had been her intention, and when he'd reached the shops, managed to lose her by joining a throng of people and hiding in a bookshop.

The letters became more critical and abusive, and the next time he was aware of being followed, he waited for her. She didn't try to evade him, and believing she wanted to be recognised, he approached her.

'Just what is it you want?' he asked, avoiding using her name. Peremptory. He knew he must have sounded threatening.

'You know what I want,' she answered, reaching out for him, seemingly surprised by the question, and sounding as sweet as she could. 'And by the way, Derek is jealous.'

'Why should Derek be jealous?' Ed was getting annoyed.

'My husband…he thinks you like me,' she said knowingly. 'He knows you like me.'

'But I don't, Berice, I don't! Not like you think.' He turned and hastened away.

Such a response should have left no room for doubt about his feelings, but Berice was not deterred. Her letter that arrived the next day accused him of not treating her as a lady should be treated, restated her love for him and complained that he hadn't admitted his love for her.

Lucy was annoyed, not with Ed's ignoring of the mad woman's advances, because she understood his reasons for doing so, but because the woman would not take no for an answer.

As luck would have it, she saw Berice the following day creeping towards the letterbox, clutching a letter and hoping not to be seen. Ed had described her tangle of black hair. It could be no one else. It was late afternoon when it was still half-light, and dying shadows fingered the ground. Ed wasn't home.

Lucy waited till she was close by and raced outside to confront her. Berice had reached the letter box and saw her coming, but it was too late to turn and run, not that she had any intention of doing so. She stood her ground, a dirty envelope in her hand, already defiant.

Lucy looked at her quarry for several seconds as if she might glean some understanding from her appearance. Berice returned the stare. A brief stand-off.

'Not another letter for my husband, is it?' Lucy said accusingly. She hadn't meant to sound aggressive but the other woman's combative pose angered her. 'I thought you would have got the message by now. My husband,' and Lucy accented the word 'husband', 'is not interested in you.'

'So you're the wife.' Berice met accusation with hostility. 'Not at all what I imagined. No, not at all. I thought you'd be pretty. I can understand now why Ed has such an interest in me.'

Lucy was furious but changed tack, hiding her emotion. Reason rather than accusation. Hostility only breeds hostility. 'Look, Berice,' she tried to sound reasonable, 'Ed and I are happily married, and you have a husband you say is jealous. Can't you see that you're hurting him? Wouldn't it be the best thing all round for you to pay more attention to your own husband rather than someone else's?'

'I can't help it if your husband is showing more interest in me than in you.' Berice countered reason with her own brand of logic. Her own husband wasn't mentioned.

'I'm telling you, he's not interested in you. In fact, he thinks…' Lucy paused.

'What? What does he think!' Berice yelled, then suddenly quietened and smiled. 'Yes, yes of course, I know what you're trying to do. You don't fool me. I know exactly what he thinks…and what he feels.'

Lucy finally understood the futility of argument. 'If you don't leave us alone, and we have every one of your ridiculous letters as proof, I'll call in the police.'

Berice was obviously thrown by hearing that Lucy knew about the letters, and might even have read them. She called them ridiculous. 'You rotten bastard,' she screamed, her face contorted, and moved a pace towards Lucy still screaming obscenities. She raised her hand to slap Lucy's face.

But Lucy was too quick. She swerved out of the way, turned and half-ran to the house, not out of cowardice, but to avoid a very public scuffle. There was no reason to stand toe to toe with this woman. It would be demeaning to do so.

*

Once married, Lucy was keen to continue working, and accepted a position at a large firm of commercial printers. The work wasn't demanding, and when a position was advertised after a few months for a personal assistant to the boss, Mr Ellis, Ed convinced her to apply. The ad gave a detailed job description, and concluded by saying that the successful applicant would need excellent organisational and interpersonal skills.

'You'd be good at all those things,' Ed said. 'You keep saying that what you're doing now is boring.'

'But there might be internal applicants,' Lucy answered. 'I've only been there for a little while. Some people have been in the company for years.'

Lucy was encouraged by Ed's support and applied. So did Anne

Keating. She was a very large, barrel-shaped woman with stick-thin legs she hid by wearing slacks. She had a doughy face that became red and perspired when she was angry, and that was a lot of the time. She'd been with the company for nine years. Photos of her as a woman in her late teens revealed a smiling and not unattractive woman with a slightly horsey face reclaimed by long raven hair and a good figure. The years had recharactered her face so that people were likely to remark, 'I wouldn't want to get on the wrong side of her!' And her figure had grown, the flesh disappearing from her thighs and gathering in her stomach, perhaps over-indulgence or unhappiness.

Do all stories have a beginning and an end? For Anne Keating, they did. The past is a fertile place for imagined beginnings. And reasons, and excuses. If Anne had to name a beginning for her sorry narrative, it would be her end of school formal, or was it simply a case of blame's retrospective tendency to magnify itself, the curse of failed hopes?

Woody, an affectionate nickname for one of the girls' favourites among the boys, agreed to take her to the formal. She'd asked him one Friday after school and he'd accepted. If there'd been an independent observer, the exchange would have been reported as Anne saying casu-ally as she hurried out the school gate, 'It would be really nice to go to the formal together,' and Woody, also in a hurry, replying, 'Yes, that'd be good.'

For Anne, Woody's answer was a commitment set in cement, and she excitedly began selecting a dress and discussing with her mother whether she needed a new pair of shoes and how she should wear her hair. Her father was enlisted to drive them to and from. They were the days when very few senior students could boast having a car.

With a little hubris, she told the girls at school, believing it would be seen as a conquest that would improve her status. Woody was a prize. She didn't see the surprised looks they exchanged, or the whisperings behind hands. In the week leading up to the formal, she spent hours in her room, lying on the bed, imagining romantic scenarios, believing it was the start of something special.

The dream was shattered the day before the event when she spoke to Woody to tell him her father would drive them. Woody's face blanched and he looked at her with his mouth open. She knew something was wrong. His reaction could only mean one thing. She waited. Thoughts banged in her head like marbles in a tin can.

'But Anne,' he stammered, recalling their talk a couple of Fridays ago, 'I don't think we really agreed…' He left it at that, chastened by the hurt and anger in her face.

'We certainly did,' she said softly. 'We agreed.'

There was silence for several seconds.

'But it wasn't definite,' he managed to say.

'It was very definite,' she said more aggressively, and then more quietly, 'We are going together aren't we, Woody?' She stressed the 'are', but realised the futility of the question.

'I've asked Felicity,' he said more assuredly.

'But I've…' She started and stopped. She wanted to tell him about all the trouble she'd gone to, but would a boy understand what a girl does to prepare for such an occasion?

'I'm sorry about the misunderstanding,' Woody said lamely.

'You damn well ought to be. How could you?' she said spitefully. No point pleading now. Might as well let fly. 'What sort of person are you?'

'I never agreed,' he said loudly. Contrition had morphed into attack. Better for him to assume the moral high ground.

Did it colour, or poison, her dealings with the opposite sex after that? Her frequent mulling over it suggested that she had allowed it to fester over the years. The sniggering of a few of the girls who'd known for days, and delighted in her humiliation, created a more general mistrust of people.

Since then, there'd been a long succession of disappointments: two failed relationships, a financial setback, her father leaving home, and her failure to secure acting roles after her two years of training at the National Institute for Dramatic Art. Directors avoided talking of her acting ability, saying that she didn't quite fit the role. Not sweet or naïve enough for Ophelia, and not witty or caustic enough for a Mrs Warren.

She became gradually more bitter, more resentful of those who enjoyed greater success and more happiness. At times, her ill feeling toward the world turned to pleasure when a tall poppy was brought down to earth, or when someone suffered an undeserved fate.

How long will I go on being trodden under foot? I won't allow the bastards to get me down, she'd begun to swear. My time will come. Just you wait. Someone will pay.

*

Anne had already persuaded two other women not to apply for the advertised position, convincing them they had no chance, and the day before the interview, knowing that Lucy would not be subject to the same intimidation, she took a report from Lucy's desk when she had gone home, a report that Lucy had written and typed for Bob Ellis, retyped it to include numerous spelling and grammatical errors, and returned it to Lucy's out tray. It would be on Bob's desk early the next morning.

Despite Anne's best efforts at sabotage, Lucy was given the position, and Anne was incensed. She excoriated Lucy to her work colleagues, not caring if Lucy heard.

'Have you seen how Ellis looks at her,' she'd say. 'It's sickening. Oh Lucy, would you mind,' she mimicked sarcastically. 'She got the job because he likes her. It had nothing to do with ability. What else do you do for him, Lucy?'

It was while slating Lucy that an idea occurred to her. After a few days, she typed a letter:

Dear Mr Ellis,

I wanted to thank you for making me your personal assistant. I've admired you in my short time here.

My admiration and, dare I say it, my affection for you have

increased since we've been working closely together. I look forward to coming to work, and being able to lighten your load in any way I can.

I apologise if I'm being too forward, but hope you may feel a little of the same.

Yours, Lucy.

She was excited by her efforts and made sure the letter was placed in Mr Ellis's in tray.

The next day, a serious-looking Bob Ellis called Lucy into his office and closed the door. She could tell that something was afoot.

'I read your letter,' he started, looking shy, and waited for Lucy to say something.

'Which one, Mr Ellis?' Lucy answered innocently. She'd already typed several that morning.

'Your letter, and please call me Bob.' He waited again.

Lucy didn't know what he was talking about. No letter she'd typed was any more hers than another.

Bob Ellis, believing Lucy might have been embarrassed at revealing her feelings, decided to take the initiative. It was his turn to answer if not confess. 'Lucy, you said in your letter that you hoped I felt a little of the same.' He paused, swallowed. 'I do. I liked you from the first day you came here.' He was perspiring, and fidgeting with his pen and the stapler on his desk, looking towards the floor as he spoke.

'Mr Ellis, I mean Bob,' Lucy replied in a state of confusion, but seeing a way clear, 'do you have the letter…the one I…wrote?'

Bob reached into his drawer and handed her the letter. Her fingers were trembling as she took it from its envelope. As she read it, her mouth open in surprise and shock, Bob realised that she wasn't the author.

They were silent for a minute. It was an awkward situation. Bob had declared his affection for her, and it was too late to withdraw his admission. Lucy liked him, but like was all. But from the way Bob reacted, could it be more than simply being fond of her? There'd been nothing else in his behaviour to suggest it was anything more.

How could she rescue him, help him save face? Some of Anne's letter was the truth. She admired him and wanted to lighten his load. She felt nothing more, but it would be hurtful for him if she dismissed even that.

Bob hadn't moved from behind the desk. 'I think I've made a fool of myself,' he said, and he looked at her attentively, waiting for her to take the lead.

She did. 'I think we both know now, Bob,' she began slowly, and hesitated, 'that I didn't write the letter, and that someone was trying to embarrass and hurt me, hurt us both.' She paused, watching his reaction. 'I am fond of you, and I'm grateful that you've told me of your feelings.'

'You needn't say anything more, Lucy,' he answered and lapsed again into silence.

But Lucy felt the need to press on. A thing as important as this couldn't be left up in the air. 'We're both embarrassed, but why should we be?' She tried to sound upbeat. 'There's nothing wrong with two people saying they like each other. Perfectly natural. If I didn't like you, I wouldn't have applied for the job.'

She opened the door gently, and left the office, knowing she must have looked a deathly white. When she passed Anne's desk, she saw her grinning.

'Everything all right, Lucy?' she said with feigned innocence. There was no doubt who had written the letter.

She struggled through the rest of the day. Bob didn't call on her once, and his office door was closed. Anne was gloating.

Lucy was relieved when she wasn't dismissed the following day.

Bob was relaxed when he spoke to her, and told her that he'd thought a lot about what she'd said about there being nothing wrong with two people saying they were fond of each other. 'Two people working together should like each other,' he said. 'We won't let it spoil our work relationship, Lucy,' he added. 'It's no longer awkward for me, and I hope it isn't for you. And by the way, you got the job on merit. You were by far the best applicant.'

He also told her that it was obvious who had written the letter, and that he knew the report she'd written and typed had been tampered with. 'You never make a spelling mistake,' he said. 'If there'd only been one or two, it might have been more believable, but there were a dozen, and the grammar wasn't worthy of an infants' schoolchild.

She walked from the office feeling exuberant. She'd had a restless night thinking of what it meant for her future. Anne's glee turned to concern as Lucy passed.

And the concern turned to anxiety an hour later when she was called into Bob's office. She was only there for a minute before she walked out swearing loudly and began to throw files across the room, and empty her desk of her personal possessions. The office workers watched silently, wary of commenting or laughing lest they become a target for the missile pens and staplers.

'Just you wait,' she snarled at Lucy as she left. 'Make no mistake, you haven't heard the end of this.' Her face was full of hate.

*

'I know we've asked before, but we have to know about anyone who might have felt hostile towards you, or your wife,' Ken began when Ed had queried why they needed to speak to him again.

Ken and Kane were sitting on one side of a large table while he sat on the other side. He would have preferred Clive and his less formal manner.

'We've read the letters and notes you were sent by a Mrs Berice Downing. In the latter ones, she seemed to be getting very annoyed with you.' Ken stopped and looked at him searchingly.

'We know you had nothing to do with her,' Kane added, thinking he was putting Ed at his ease, 'that you didn't encourage her.'

'It's all in the letters,' Ed answered. 'One crazy woman's imagination. I don't know what else I can add. Even the letters make it clear that I gave her no encouragement, none at all. I didn't go to any of her meeting dates. And I don't know of anyone who might feel hostile towards me. I always try to please, avoid confronting people. Too much so, Lucy says.' He looked away, visibly upset. 'Said,' he added quietly.

'Did your wife ever have any communication with this woman, at least any that you know about?' Ken resumed.

'We don't have any secrets,' Ed replied, 'but yes, Lucy caught her at our letter box, tried to reason with her, and when she couldn't, threatened to go to the police if she didn't stop harassing me.'

Ken and Kane looked at each other and nodded. Kane took notes.

'What was this woman's reaction to your wife's threat?' Ken asked.

'When Lucy said she knew about the letters, the woman probably assumed she had read them. She went wild, screamed obscenities, went for Lucy to hit her…it brought the neighbours out on the street.'

'She assaulted your wife?'

Both men were alert, watching Ed closely.

'Wanted to, tried to, but Lucy retreated before she could. Went inside. The woman started punching and kicking the letter box, trying to knock it off its post. I think she hurt her hand. Screamed for Lucy to come back out.'

'And how did she treat you after that? Ken asked. 'Showing your wife her letters, something that personal…couldn't have pleased her. Did she try to assault you too.'

'No, it was the husband who did the assaulting.'

'What!' Ken nearly leapt from his chair.

Kane was even more alert than normal.

'The husband assaulted her?'

'No. He assaulted me. Was waiting for me on the way home. Screamed at me to keep away from his wife, and knocked me down. Wanted me to get up and fight.'

'And did you?' Ken asked.

'No. He's built like a tank. And it wouldn't have proven anything. Besides, two women came by and saw what he wanted to do…saved me from having my head kicked in.'

'Did you report it to the police?' Kane asked.

'Yes. Lucy insisted. I probably wouldn't have. I wasn't hurt. Only my pride. They're both crazies. Anyway, the letters stopped.'

'Why haven't we heard about it?' It was more a statement to Kane than a question. 'The boys in homicide are always the last to hear.' Ken was annoyed. 'Clive will be furious.'

'Why didn't you tell us, Mr Grainger? Didn't you think it might be relevant, that it might have some bearing on what happened to your wife?'

'No, I didn't. The whole messy business was about me, and not about Lucy.'

'It seems to me that it became your wife's problem too…a woman furious that her love letters had been shared, and mad enough to attack her.' Ken was irritated. 'And a man who knocked you down and wanted to go on with it, convinced you were going after his wife. Did you really never think…'

'Is there anyone else who might have had reason to hurt your wife?' Kane asked after half a minute's awkward silence.

'There was a woman at Lucy's work who was really bitter when Lucy was promoted instead of her. Made trouble and got herself fired. Made threats to Lucy…but surely not the sort of thing you'd want to kill someone for, if that's what you're thinking.'

Ken wanted to tell him to leave the decisions about what was important to them, but he thought better of it.

Just his mention of the word 'kill' stoked painful memories for Ed, and he retreated into himself. The interview continued for another ten minutes.

'Anything useful?' Clive later asked.

'A few things we should follow up,' Ken answered. 'There's more to this Berice story than we were led to believe. A lot more.'

Both men were hopeful it might lead somewhere.

6

The death of Lucy's father had been a shock. He'd had a massive heart attack that claimed him without warning when he was entertaining friends. Lucy, as the youngest child had been his favourite, his 'little girl' who could do no wrong, and she regretted not having seen him for six weeks before he was taken.

She'd become a frequent visitor to her mother, who had suffered a decline from the recent loss, and after several months she asked Lucy for her help with several matters relating to property, trusts and other assets that required legal help after her father's death.

'I wouldn't know where to start,' she told Lucy tearfully. 'And as for your brothers… What can I do?'

Lucy naturally agreed, though she was resentful that neither of her brothers would accept the responsibility. Owen was willing to help, but he was a little 'challenged', and she could understand his reluctance. He'd be confused. It was beyond him, but her other brother, Simon, used the demands of his wife and two children as an excuse. He believed Lucy didn't have his business acumen, but she'd at least be thorough, and that's all Simon believed was necessary.

'I haven't been married for long myself,' she wanted to tell Simon. 'Do you think I've nothing to do?' But she didn't want to cause her already anxious mother any more stress by creating a family feud. Her mother wasn't coping with the bereavement, and Lucy was fearful that her father's death had been the catalyst for something more serious.

Lucy googled lawyers in her locality, and settled on Adrian Passmore and Associates, a small firm of six lawyers nearby who specialised in conveyancing, and handled all civil matters except for criminal law.

Ed asked if she would like him to go with her, but she wasn't stressed, believing that she could give the lawyers all the documents and correspondence, and let them settle the matter. She felt she needed to do this alone for her father's sake. And the more she thought about it, the better she felt about this final gesture. He'd be pleased. His little girl.

A very attractive secretary greeted her in a tastefully decorated foyer and introduced herself as Blanche. 'Mr Passmore is expecting you,' she said in a dulcet voice and gestured towards the nearest door. Her nails flashed red, and her teeth were white in the bright neon lighting. She watched Lucy moving to the door.

*

There was never a better example of success breeding success than in Adrian Passmore. He had the good fortune of being born to wealthy parents who were determined not to spoil him but to ensure that he didn't go without what would secure him and his younger brother contented and profitable futures.

His father possessed a military image of 'a man' which his elder son delighted in fulfilling. Apart from instilling a code of manly and courtly behaviour, it involved playing rugby in the firsts for St Josephs, an elite private school for boys that enjoyed a long history of success in producing future players in the national team.

There were better academics, but he was good enough to gain a place to study law at Sydney University. He passed but with no real distinction. The confinement coupled with the sexual obsessiveness of the school boarders, led to a beyond-school time of limited social and sexual experimentation that distracted him from his studies. His doting parents looked on, his mother with pride and anxiety, and his father with a knowing, perhaps an approving, smile. It wasn't inconsistent with his image of a man.

Despite the mediocre academic record, he was given a position in a small but highly regarded law firm, and was quick to prove his worth, both in attracting clients, and in achieving satisfactory results for them. There was something to be said for the old school tie.

He met Stella, the daughter of financial adviser friends of his father. 'Stella by name and stellar by nature,' he'd later tell his friends. A graduate of Ravenswood Girls', an elite girls' school in the northern suburbs, and the University of New South Wales, there was no chemistry at first, but both their families were keen on the match, and construing shared interests as the be-all of relationship and marital happiness, called them 'kindred spirits'. They grew closer to each other, though it's hard to say how much of their growing fondness and commitment was fashioned for them.

Their marriage, a grand affair, made the fashion pages of newspapers and magazines. A boy and a girl followed in quick succession, and they settled into a contented and privileged life, both pursuing careers, yet being caring and responsible parents.

His early good looks hadn't faded with time. He was a tall, conventionally handsome man with a slim figure in his early forties who wore self-assurance as a professional badge. He had a full head of slate-grey hair, a pronounced dimple in the middle of his chin, and an ever-present, sometimes ironic smile.

Blanche Louvier, Adrian's secretary, did not share his or Stella's privileged origins. A graduate of a state high school in the underprivileged west of the state, she attended secretarial school, where she excelled at shorthand and typing. Determined to get ahead, she also took elocution and deportment classes.

The pressure to succeed often produced anxiety which a therapist diagnosed as 'anxiety disorder'. At her interview, she shared the news with Adrian, who was impressed by her honesty. It was better that he knew. Her insomnia, a general characteristic of anxiety disorder, didn't affect her work, but there could be times of irritability, fatigue, restlessness and difficulty concentrating. She didn't tell him about another common feature of anxiety disorder, a fixation on the imagined outcomes of some scenarios.

She was put on probation, proved to be good at her work, and Adrian believed having such an attractive woman in the front office was a winning introduction to the firm.

*

'Come in, Mrs Grainger.' Adrian Passmore had come out from behind his desk to open the door and shake her hand. 'Please,' and he stood aside, pointing to a leather-studded settee.

'Mr Passmore. Thank you for seeing me at such short notice.'

'Adrian, please, Mrs Grainger, and may I call you…' he glanced at his record of appointments, 'Lucy?'

Lucy smiled. She already felt at ease. This was a man who was practised in the art of making people feel comfortable.

'How can I help you?' he asked. His smile was infectious.

Lucy took a large file of correspondence from her bag. 'When my father passed away a few weeks ago…' she began, and felt suddenly emotional. The tears started to flow. She'd been shocked when her father had died, but she hadn't cried, not like this. It was as if the grief had been silently accumulating, biding its time, growing in intensity and waiting for a trigger, the right word, a kind face, a poignant vision or a trivial incident.

Adrian wasn't fazed. He hesitated for half a minute before he took her hand and waited for the tears to stop. It was forward for a lawyer-client relationship, but it felt appropriate under the circumstances and she didn't seem to mind.

'Sorry. I'm so embarrassed,' Lucy said, drying her eyes and withdrawing her hand. 'I can just imagine what you're thinking. Another silly emotional female. It's not at all like me. And what do they say about blondes?' She laughed.

'Not at all,' Adrian answered. 'Another rare and caring female.' He wasn't smiling, and he certainly knew the right thing to say.

It didn't take Lucy long to explain the little she knew about what needed to be done. She had copies of the will and investment portfolios, and the names of associates.

Adrian nodded, taking each of the documents in turn as Lucy finished. 'Give me a week to sort through this material,' he said, and he called Blanche on the intercom to discuss appointment times. 'It's been a real pleasure, Lucy,' and he held her hand for several seconds before she left.

'I don't know how I'll be able to face him again,' she told Ed, giving an account of the meeting. 'It was so embarrassing. If he'd produced a white handkerchief when I started to howl, the cliché would have been complete.'

'I'm quite sure you've no need to be embarrassed,' Ed assured her. 'He must see a lot of that, and besides, he called you caring. That says heaps about the way he sees you.'

Their second meeting a week later took place after she'd finished at work. Adrian didn't mind. It was his suggestion. He needed to stay back to finish preparation for a meeting with his colleagues the following day.

They sat on the same settee and Adrian explained what had needed to be done, and how he'd acted on the matters. Lucy didn't want to hear the details. All she needed to know was that nothing else had to be done, that it had been taken out of her hands. But for Adrian, professional accountability demanded that he give a full account. And he wanted to impress.

When he'd finally finished, he asked her how she was coping with her grief. He didn't always show this much concern with his other clients. It was really none of his business, and it might have been frowned upon by his colleagues. But there was something about her.

She smiled, knowing he was alluding to her tears at their last meeting, told him she was still embarrassed by what had happened because it was so unlike her, and thanked him for his understanding.

'Please don't feel embarrassed,' he told her. 'It was a perfectly natural reaction.' He stood.

There were a few seconds of pregnant silence. The meeting was over.

'Thank you, Adrian,' she said, offering him her hand.

The use of his Christian name surprised him, even though he had asked her to use it at their first meeting. It seemed to give a new dimension to their relationship.

On her way to the door, the strap of one of her half-heel shoes broke, and she was stumbling when Adrian caught and righted her.

'Are you all right?' he asked with obvious concern. But he didn't let go.

Neither did she.

They made love on the leather-studded settee.

In the days to come, she would relive those few minutes over and over, not so much to dwell on the pleasure of it, and it was pleasurable, but to ask herself why. It had never entered her thoughts. She hadn't lusted after him, at least not in any conscious sense.

She knew that sex could be a dispassionate agreement to satisfy a natural need with an agreeable partner. It certainly wasn't that. It was frequently a frenzied grappling and hurried discarding of clothes to satisfy a lust that needed urgent quenching. It wasn't like that. Sometimes it was the result of an incremental creep of desire over time with an assumed conclusion. It wasn't like that either.

She hadn't thought about him since their first meeting. Was there some deep unsatisfied emotional need in people that craved a tangible expression, one they were not aware of, let alone able to articulate? One that flamed and was just as quickly extinguished.

She remembered getting up from the settee, fully dressed from the waist up, her blouse crushed and twisted, her naked buttocks peeling from the leather. She remembered his long, hairless white legs, and his discarded pinstripe trousers lying on the floor. She remembered them dressing slowly in silence and, once dressed, speaking tenderly to each other, not with words of love that might be expected, because there was no love, and not with promises of repeating their lovemaking, but with words that might be used when two people realise something special has happened.

At the time, she felt no guilt. It seemed the natural thing to do. So natural she didn't see it as a betrayal. She kissed him on the cheek when she left, a bloodless kiss that she might have given to a girlfriend's partner. There was no passionate farewell. No declarations.

She wasn't stricken with remorse when she returned to Ed, and treated him with the same caring that she always did. She did lie in bed that night and think of what had happened, but more with curiosity than misgiving. Ed made no move towards her, and as he purred softly in his sleep beside her, she leant over and kissed his cheek. He murmured but didn't wake up.

She had a second meeting with Adrian a week later at the same time to complete their business. He greeted her warmly with an outstretched hand as if nothing had happened between them, and when they completed their business, they embraced like old friends, quickly moving apart when there was a rustling noise in the front office and a sound like someone clearing their throat.

They made love again, not with urgency but with more finesse. They were both naked, and took turns doing what gave each other pleasure. It may have been this more calculated sex, its deliberate and continued intent, perhaps its premeditation as opposed to the spontaneous lovemaking of the week before, that troubled Lucy. It seemed to cross some boundary, though she wasn't sure what it was. Had it moved from a more excusable expression of urgent need to a less excusable planned affair?

She had to admit that she had enjoyed it, but knew that it couldn't go on. It wasn't even a matter of denying herself. She really didn't want it to happen again. She'd begun to feel guilty, guilt at what she had done, perhaps an affront to decency, loyalty, fidelity, morality, even convention. They dressed hurriedly and in silence.

Adrian could sense the sudden change. 'I know,' he said, reading her face and her thoughts, after they had dressed and she was thinking of what to say.

'You understand,' she answered. 'I knew you would.' It was a statement rather than a question. 'Do you feel the same?' She believed he did.

They were standing, facing each other.

He shrugged rather than nodded. 'Perhaps it's for the best,' he answered.

There was no further discussion. Knowledge can be dramatic and intuitive, not needing words.

She kissed him on the cheek as she left like she had on the previous occasion, and thanked him for all he had done. And she meant it.

'I'll send the probate details as soon as they come,' he called after her.

She smiled. Things had returned to the strictly professional. How fickle people are. And how resilient. It was almost as if nothing had happened.

Over the next few weeks, her guilt became remorse, but she decided to say nothing about it to Ed. He would battle to accept it, and the damage to their marriage was not worth the risk. And she wasn't sure what defence she could give if she did say something, when she wasn't sure herself why it had happened.

The stock reason for people having an affair is that they are unhappy in their present relationship. If they are happy, the conventional wisdom says, there'd be no reason to stray. This puzzled her. She was very happy with Ed. She loved him, and she was no sexual novice and no sexual fly-by-night, so why Adrian? The argument that she was experimenting, testing her emotional and sexual limits, didn't have any weight. Nor did the notion that she was trying to free herself from the constraints or conventions of marriage. She had all the freedom she wanted. And she loved Ed.

She had to hurry to the bedroom when she returned from Adrian the second time, when Ed had asked her if she was all right, looking at her curiously. He was so trusting. The thought of what happened with Adrian would never have occurred to him. Did he notice the rumpled clothes, smell the aftermath of sex, or another man's aftershave?

And he probably didn't notice how much more attentive she was to his needs in the weeks that followed. She resolved that she would be the best wife possible, not that she hadn't been, but that never, never again…

Two evenings after her last meeting with Adrian, she received an anonymous call. It was a woman, hushed, and while she tried to disguise her voice, it seemed to be educated, affected.

'I know what you're doing,' the voice said accusingly. There was a pause, rapid breathing, the sound of a door opening.

'Who is this?' Lucy asked, alarmed, indignant.

There was a further pause, a man's voice in the background, and the phone went dead.

Lucy was shaken. Someone must know and, if so, there was no telling what they might do. It could bring her world crashing down around her. Might this person want money? Was blackmail the motive? But there was nothing she could do. She could only hope there'd be no more calls.

She debated whether to tell Adrian, and decided against it. He would be no wiser than she was, and might even suspect her motive.

*

Ed had experienced a good few months. Lucy was very attentive and their relationship had reached new heights. They shared the little vulnerabilities that people cling to and often never reveal, the fears, humilities and insecurities. Lucy had been promoted at work, and they visited the cinema and theatre. He went to a ballroom dancing class with her and made a fool of himself. It became instant folklore. She went to a rugby league game and needed everything explained. That became joking dinner table conversation with friends. Their lovemaking was frequent and tender.

Their only real challenge was Berice. It was during this time that Lucy had her altercation with Berice at the letterbox. They didn't allow the sour taste it left to last for long, and Lucy sweetened its effect with her own brand of light-heartedness:

'I don't suppose we can be too hard on her,' she said, 'for falling madly in love with you.'

'No, I suppose not,' Ed replied, winking. 'I suppose I'm irresistible.'

He had been walking home from shopping when he noticed a man following him. He was a big man, overweight, making little effort to conceal his movements. Ed had made a sudden turn, and started to walk on a circular track that later joined the main track a hundred metres further back. For a few seconds, he thought he'd lost the man, but he reappeared and was even closer than before.

So, to be sure of the man's intentions, Ed began to jog. The man kept pace, but was breathing heavily. There was no doubting his intentions now. Ed was considering running ahead and leaving him well behind, when the man called out, and as Ed stopped on hearing his name, the man caught up.

'Ed Grainger?' the man said again.

'Yes.'

Ed turned to face the man, and was hit in the face. He didn't see it coming. No time for evasive action. It was a savage punch to the side of his head and he lost his balance and fell to the ground. His head spun. The left side of his mouth felt like a wet tingling sponge. It took him several seconds to recover.

The man stood over him, punching the fist of one hand into the open palm of the other. He was not tall, but very solid, with tattooed wrestler's arms that hung further than normal at his sides like those of Neanderthal man. He had a raw face, beady close-together eyes and dark bushy eyebrows. 'Get up you bastard,' he shouted, 'and fight like a man, or I'll give you a bloody good kicking.'

Ed remained on the ground, supporting himself on an elbow. He wasn't badly hurt but knew the side of his mouth was bleeding, wondered if some teeth were loose. The man was wearing a ring that had torn his cheek. He had no intention of standing. He wasn't a coward, but he knew when he'd met his match, and what purpose would fighting serve?

It only occurred to him later that if he had been stupid enough to fight the man, it might be seen by both husband and wife as a contest for Berice. Is that what she wanted? Knights duelling for her favours? The man looked like he'd been in more than a few scraps, and he was relishing this one, waiting to knock Ed down again.

'What…' Ed began to say, suspecting but not knowing who the man was.

But there was no need for questions. The answer was instant.

'Bloody keep away from my wife,' the man shouted, standing with one leg either side of Ed's body like a colossus.

Ed knew the greatest danger would be to provoke the man. He knew now who it was, and thought he would probably be as deaf to reason as his wife. There was no knowing what fiction Berice had told him.

'Last chance,' Derek roared. 'Get up and fight like a man, or I'll kick your head in.' He readied for a kick, and Ed could see the hobnail workman's boots.

'Are you all right?' he heard a timid voice.

Ed didn't move, but was aware of two women who took the same route home from work as him, standing on the path and watching timidly.

Derek saw them too, and thought better of launching into a full attack. 'Be warned, you bastard,' he snarled and moved away. 'What do you think you're looking at?' He made a menacing gesture towards the women, who flinched but stood their ground and continued to watch from the path. Beating up men was acceptable, but attacking women was not even part of his code.

Ed was fortunate that the two witnesses were not intimidated by Derek, and were willing to support his account to the police.

He told them the full story, detailing his first bizarre meeting with Berice, the stalking and the letters, the threats, or were they meant to be enticements, the claim that Derek was jealous, and his meeting with Derek in the park.

The police were sceptical, but when, after the witnesses gave their account, they visited the Downings' home, they were soon convinced. Berice and Derek shouted, contradicted each other, and made ridiculous accusations. Berice professed her love for Ed, insisted that he felt the same, and was slapped hard across the face by her husband, who had to be restrained.

'They're nuts,' an officer told Ed.

The letters stopped soon afterwards.

A few days later, Ed had a dream. Because he so rarely dreamt, he found it disturbing:

'Now be very careful,' his mother said to the young Ed. She was dressed in a cerise suit, and her hair was attractively styled. 'Lucy can't swim, so it's up to you to make sure she's all right. You will be careful, won't you,' and she patted him on the head.

Lucy was excited about going to the beach. They'd been going a lot recently, and it always made her animated. She felt a free spirit. It was part of the ritual to put sunscreen on before they left. He had to cream her back for her. Her face was so plastered in hot-pink zinc that it covered her freckles and disguised her good looks. She looked boyish.

When they arrived at the beach, they dropped their towels together somewhere between the flags, and headed for the surf at a run. Lucy led the way, and he watched her bounding into the water and diving under the first wave. He followed close behind.

It had never been so good. The water was cool but not icy, and the waves were big enough to be a challenge, but not so big that they were dumpers. They swam, jumped and rode waves for half an hour before Lucy, her eyes gleaming, swam further out. He remembered that his mother had said Lucy couldn't swim.

He was pleasantly tired and returned to shore to lie on his towel and feel the sun drying the water on his back. The beach was still crowded. The heat was soporific and he dropped off to sleep. When he woke up, he didn't know how long he'd been asleep. It could have been an hour. It might only have been minutes. He felt groggy.

Lucy hadn't returned, and he walked to the water's edge to see if he could spot her in the water. He wasn't concerned. The beach was still crowded and he couldn't see her, so he returned to lie down on his towel.

The afternoon wore on, and people began to leave. Eventually, there were only a dozen people in the water. Lucy wasn't one of them.

He waited until an orange sunset blazed across the water, and the sea was the colour of graphite. Lucy's towel wasn't where she'd left it, so it seemed likely that she had returned home with the towel wrapped around her wet costume. But why hadn't she told him?

He arrived home and called her name. There was no answer. He went to the bedroom, and his mother was lying in his bed. She looked at him strangely as if she didn't know who he was. Her eyes looked startled, her face was creased, and her hair was a mess of stringy grey.

'Is Lucy here, Mum?' he asked.

'Who do you think you are, bursting into a lady's bedroom?' she said indignantly, sitting up in the bed.

'Mum, it's me, Ed, your son.'

His mother looked at him through rheumy eyes. 'I haven't got a son,' she said with disgust, and in the same breath, 'now get out of here or I'll find out who you are and get your father to give you a good spanking.'

7

A positive result meant that both lines, the testing line and the control line, would turn pink within a few minutes. She'd already added a little of her sample to the specially treated strip on the pregnancy stick. Now all she could do was wait.

She'd bought the home pregnancy test a week after her missed period. She was always very regular, so there was some reason for alarm. But there were no cramps and her breasts weren't hurting.

She wondered whether to stay with her eyes glued to the stick, her anxiety getting out of control, or busy herself as a diversion for a few minutes. She decided on the latter, but didn't go far away. She began to dust the two bedside tables and the lamps, finding it hard to concentrate.

Ed hadn't been told. They'd joked about the patter of little feet, but hadn't seriously discussed having a child, and while she was certain he'd be pleased, she wasn't sure what she felt about it. She wanted children, but she would have preferred to wait a few years. She would have to tell Ed at some stage if the test was positive. She might wait and tell him when she'd been to a gynaecologist and there was no doubt. Couldn't these home kits be wrong sometimes?

She finished the dusting that didn't need doing, and turned her attention to the pregnancy stick lying on the bed. Both lines were turning pink. She kept watching. She had to be sure. It might be illusion, lighting cast from the bedside lamp, or imagination. But as she watched, the pink became bolder. She was pregnant.

She felt awe and shock, and put the test away at the bottom of her drawer of underwear. Ed would never look in there.

But apart from the timing of the pregnancy, that they hadn't planned, there was a more powerful reason for her shock, and her need to keep her testing a secret. There was no way of knowing whether the baby was Ed's or Adrian's. She counted back the days in her cycle and realised her timing with Adrian couldn't have been worse. She'd been so stupid not using protection. It was almost certainly Ed's, but how could she be sure?

She lay face down on the bed, her head cradled by her crossed arms, and muttered aloud, 'What to do, what to do? Please God, make it go away.' She stayed that way for several minutes, but knowing that feeling sorry for herself would achieve nothing, she put on her running gear and left the house. It was her tried and true method of clearing her head.

The effort would not normally tire her. It did now. The shock had taken its toll on her body. She sat in the park, watching a mother playing with her infant child. The little girl had curly mid-brown hair, pink cheeks and chubby legs. She was wearing a dress of red polka dots on white, with white socks and sandals.

'Let me do it, Mummy,' she said when her mother tried to carry her to the top of the slippery dip, and she climbed the steps laboriously and sat at the top with a smile. 'I told you I could do it, Mummy. Watch. Watch me,' and she slid down to where her mother stopped her from tumbling forward when she reached the ground.

Lucy watched intrigued. The little girl repeated her feat, and on the way down the slide, jammed her finger against the side. Her face crumpled and she was about to cry, but her mother saw what happened, ran to her side and lifted her into her arms.

'Mummy will kiss it better,' she said, and she did.

The little girl's face brightened instantly and she hurried for her third attempt on the slippery dip.

Lucy's hand went instinctively to her stomach. She wondered if it was the beginnings of a boy or girl in there. It wouldn't be too bad to have a little girl like the one she was watching. She could imagine herself in that mother's place. But could she manage as the little girl grew into adolescence and womanhood without knowing who her real father was? The girl would never know, and Ed would never suspect. Surely there was only a small chance that Ed wasn't the father.

Lucy continued sitting on the park bench when the mother had taken the little girl away in the pram. She tried to imagine what a little boy and girl might look like if fathered by Ed or Adrian. What if the newborn had a dimple in its chin like Adrian's?

The following fortnight was a torment for Lucy. Once the gynaecologist confirmed that the pregnancy was on its way, Ed would have to be told. But still she baulked at saying anything. She even thought of telling Adrian, but quickly dismissed the idea. He wouldn't want to know. If it ever became public, and the accusing finger was pointed at him, it would fracture his happy home life and professional reputation. And if it remained a secret, he might feel resentful and think she had engineered a planned seduction for later entrapment.

She thought of telling her mother. Mothers were supposed to be there to support their daughters with female complaints. But her mother wasn't coping with the bereavement of her husband, and a further shock might be dangerous to her mental health.

She considered a termination, but while not passionately right-to-life, she found the idea disturbing. It was premature. She had time.

Another anonymous call fractured her composure. Ed was reading the evening paper in the family room, and she considered herself lucky to have answered the phone. What might she have said to him? She didn't recognise the voice, but she did know it was the same voice as her earlier caller. It was barely a whisper, breathless and disguised.

'You'll get what's coming to you,' it said.

Again Lucy tried to engage the speaker by asking her name. 'Who are you? What do you want?'

'Bitch' was all she got before the line went dead.

'What was that about?' Ed asked, not looking up from the paper.

'Just a crank call,' she answered, trying to sound unconcerned.

This call distressed her more than the first. No one knew about the pregnancy. Could it only have been about the affair, or something else entirely? What else had she done that might earn the label of 'bastard'?

If it was about the affair, more than one person must know. And this call, unlike the first, was a threat. 'You'll get what's coming' meant something happening to her. The first carried an implicit threat, but now the threat was explicit. It seemed the threats would keep coming.

It happened one day at work with no warning, only a week after her visit to the gynaecologist. Pain. A wet feeling. Some movement low down. A hurry to the ladies' bathroom, and a rush of blood. Thankfully, no women entered the bathroom for the half hour that Lucy stayed there, so she was able to clean up, excuse herself from work on the pretext of having a migraine, and seek the necessary medical help. She was back at work pale and exhausted, but only having missed a day and a half.

She was relieved and thanked God. Perhaps the worry over the anonymous call was a contributing factor, a blessing in disguise. She wanted children now, more than ever, but with no doubts about their paternity.

Ed showed his usual concern, but was never to find out about the miscarriage. He assumed the reason for Lucy's day off work was the regular female curse.

*

She was sitting with Ed in the family room after dinner when there was a loud rapping on the door. They looked at each other to determine if either of them expected anyone. They both shook their heads. Ed went.

The opened door framed a stranger standing on the porch, a young man of eighteen or twenty, dressed in army fatigues. His black hair was shaved close to his head on both sides but not on top, his face was already burnt and weathered, and there was a tattoo of a spider in a web on his left bicep.

He stared intently at Ed before speaking. 'Ed Grainger?' he queried.

'Can I help you?' Ed answered, feeling uncomfortable with this unlikely visitor, who was obviously not a travelling salesman.

'I'm Craig, Craig Grainger,' he replied. 'Your brother, or should I say your half-brother.'

*

Craig Grainger fitted the public's profile of the disadvantaged and neglected child. He was born in Rockhampton, the love child of Ed's father and Robyn Blake, a young woman from a dysfunctional family who left school in year nine, obtained work in a sandwich shop, and then as a checkout chick in several supermarkets. Ed's father was not the first of her sexual partners, nor would he be the last.

Craig's neglect was more a matter of her ignorance than not caring. Her alcoholism and his father's indifference didn't help matters. Not long beyond his infancy, his father left the family home yet remained in Rockhampton, and Robyn found the next sexual partner in a matter of days. Ed's father had little to do with him. He was furious to learn of Robyn's pregnancy. Craig was his mother's responsibility, not his. The succession of stepfathers to follow were either indifferent or abusive.

When his mother was on a drunken binge, and there was nothing at home to eat, he resorted to stealing, mainly food, and was brought before juvenile court. His weeping mother was there with him. He was blessed with a lenient judge who spoke sternly to his mother. Things improved at home, but not for long. He resumed his stealing, but with more care, and was not beyond intimidation and assault to get what he needed. He became streetwise.

Against the odds, he finished school. 'I'm not a dummy,' was a catchcry he used with his odd assortment of down-and-out peers. He was never challenged.

He found casual work as a labourer, trawling the building sites around the city. He was strong, a good worker, and the lack of permanence suited his style of living. He could come and go as he pleased.

Before his twentieth birthday, he met Fern, and everything changed. She was a sensible girl with sound middle-class values, and where Craig was concerned, a reformist zeal. She was not the type of girl you'd have paired him with, but they never are. He fell under her spell, wanting them to live together. Her parents were opposed. They didn't see him as a desirable partner for their daughter. There was no point asking his parents.

'But Craig,' she soothed, 'where will we live? We can't be with mum and dad. You know they don't approve. They wouldn't allow it. And you don't have money for a bond and rent. Then there's food…'

'I can get a full-time job. Labouring is well paid.' He took both her hands in his own. 'It'll be enough for rent, and there'll be plenty left over.'

'You've never worked full-time. You used to say to do so would drive you mad.' She was trying to be understanding, not confronting.

'But I hadn't met you then. It's different now. I can make it work.'

'Craig,' she became suddenly serious, 'you know what Mum and Dad mean to me. I can't disobey them. If they ever agree to give us their blessing, they'll have to be convinced that I'm well provided for. No offence, but your track record is not all that impressive. It's them you have to convince, not me.'

'Then I'll convince them.'

'You won't, Craig. Believe me. If you're serious, get full-time work. We'll both save, and perhaps in a year…'

'A year!'

'All right, six months then.'

That's when Craig started to trace his never-known brother. For all he knew then, this Ed might be no better-off than himself. Their father had walked out on them too, so it was likely that they had battled like he had, and still were battling. But repeated searching of old newspapers at the public library and the internet lead to a report of Ed's marriage to a classy-looking woman, and the picture of an expensive-looking blond-brick Cape Cod home.

That's when his plan was hatched.

*

Ed was bewildered, and remained silent for several seconds, his eyes fixed on the visitor. Knowledge sometimes lags behind a sudden shock. The 'half' would have to mean a common father. 'You'd better come in.'

Lucy was open-mouthed with surprise. She had followed Ed to the door and, standing a few metres behind him, had heard the man's introduction.

The thought of turning this visitor away as an impostor didn't occur to Ed. He'd been struck by the similarity in appearance as soon as he'd opened the door. Craig looked just like Ed's father, much more than he himself did.

'Thought I'd better come and say hello,' Craig began. He'd planned the chummy beginning.

'We didn't know…' Ed wasn't sure where to start. 'Come in, come in,' and he led Craig to the sitting room, motioning to a chair.

'How could you know? Let me explain,' Craig began as he was sitting down. He seemed very sure of himself, watching Ed closely as he spoke. 'Your father met Robyn, my mother that is, almost as soon as he arrived in Rockhampton.' Craig was enjoying himself watching the confusion his arrival had created as the bearer of startling news. 'And as you can see, I'm the proud result.'

'They didn't, are they…?'

'Married…no, it didn't work out. They lived together for a while. Mum's on to number four since then.'

'And my father?' Ed asked.

He baulked at calling him 'dad'. The word carried an informality, and a fondness or familiarity he no longer felt. It was code for happy family. The pleasant memories of his early days had been replaced at first by a bitterness, and then by no feeling at all. His father might have left the house to his mother, but he had walked out when she needed him the most, without any real explanation. And he hadn't written to either of them. He was effectively dead to Ed, but this man's visit had resurrected him.

Lucy could feel Ed's discomfort and sat closer to him on the lounge, taking his hand.

'Dead,' Craig replied, and it took Ed a few seconds to realise that Craig meant it literally, to cross the line from virtual to real. He made no effort to prepare Ed for the worst, to cushion the impact. 'Four months ago. He was doing some part-time labouring on a building site, fell from scaffolding six floors up. Funny, but I always used to tell him he had two left feet.'

Craig seemed to relish telling the story. If there had once been tears, there were certainly none now. Not even a respectful manner. Ed doubted there ever had been. There was certainly nothing funny about it. No need to find something comic in two left feet when it may have been the cause of a death.

'I was there…got him the job…he used to do part-time work… didn't die straight away…he was trying to say something, a name, I think…couldn't make it out…died before he reached the hospital.' His voice didn't soften. He could have been giving a weather report.

Lucy's grip strengthened in Ed's hand. It told the story of her feelings as much as words, and he was grateful for her support. This was opening an unwelcome past, tearing away a protective covering.

'Anyway,' Craig wasn't finished, 'thought you'd appreciate knowing. I knew your names…he'd sometimes tell me something about you, Ed, so it wasn't difficult to track you down.'

'What did he say about me?' Ed asked haltingly, thinking of the time he'd spilt a little water, his father's dinner table rant, and the day they discovered he'd gone.

'You were like a stick to beat me with,' Craig laughed, but it was clear to Lucy it still rankled with him. 'Good old Ed, and bad, bad Craig.'

They were silent for a while. An answer was expected.

'Thanks, Craig,' Ed answered. 'Good of you to come.' The news had an odd impact. It should be closure of a sort, but memories of his father had been closed for Ed for many years.

Craig remained seated. He hadn't observed the time to go cue. 'Besides…' he resumed. The meeting wasn't over for him. '…there is another matter.'

Ed and Lucy raised their lowered eyes. They hadn't warmed to Craig at all. His manner was irreverent. He was too sure of himself. Another matter wasn't likely to be a pleasant matter.

'Nice house.' Craig looked at them pointedly, and made a sweeping gesture around the room. 'You've done well.'

'I beg your pardon,' Ed said, feeling the message was incomplete.

Lucy understood instantly, and started to rise, feeling hostile, but thought it better to hear the rest. She felt Ed pulling at her sleeve to sit.

'We're brothers,' Craig continued, 'we're family, we three,' and he made another gesture to include them all, 'and you have all this. My – I mean our – father,' he accented the 'our', 'told me what he left behind…'

Ed had been slow to see Craig's intent. He did now. 'Just what are you suggesting?' he asked.

'As his other son, his only other son, I believe I'm entitled, now that he's gone, to some of the assets. Aren't I a beneficiary of sorts?'

Lucy's anger was transparent. 'What!' she exclaimed and stood.

Ed tried to reason. So typical of him, Lucy thought. She wanted to throw the man out immediately. How dare he! And to bring up being the only other son, holding Ed's eyes with a meaningful stare. He must have known why it might be painful.

'But Craig, my – our – father walked out on us all those years ago to leave us to fend for ourselves. And it hasn't been easy. My mother,' and he accented the 'my', 'is the beneficiary, and if you're interested, she's still alive.'

'I know she's alive.' Craig was becoming surly. 'Our father died, and I know, I do know,' he repeated, looking at them both pointedly, 'that I am entitled to something he left behind… I know for instance that you sold the family house and used the money to buy this.' Another sweeping gesture. 'I am prepared to be reasonable…'

'Like hell,' Lucy muttered, and for a second wondered if he was telling the truth about the death of Ed's father.

Craig looked at her with hatred. He'd heard her reaction. 'Of course, if you're not prepared to cooperate, then I'll have to take it a step further.'

Ed now stood, taking Lucy's hand. 'Are you threatening us! Just what do you mean by taking it a step further?' Ed was indignant, and furious that he might be scaring Lucy. 'How dare you walk into this house and demand what isn't and never will be yours. You have no legal and certainly no moral right to make such a claim. You'd better leave right now.'

Lucy was far from scared. 'Of all the nerve,' she was outraged, 'thinking we're going to give you a purse full of money…and what will you do with it? I hate to think. Who do you think you are! Get out!' She was standing, gritting her teeth, pointing towards the door.

Craig rose slowly to his feet. He was seething. He had enjoyed the first part of the talk, seeing how uncomfortable they were, feeling Ed would be softened by hearing of his father's death, and believing that he had him over a barrel with the inheritance argument. He was wrong. 'You will regret this,' he snarled. 'Make no mistake, you will regret this,' and he left, slamming the front door.

Ed and Lucy stood silently together for half a minute. They could not remember holding each other.

Ed finally broke the silence with a typical Ed remark. 'Welcome to the family.'

Lucy gave a hint of a smile. 'Not really funny, Ed,' she said. 'That man threatened us, and he doesn't look like the type to just walk away. I think we need to take some precautions.'

They went together to the police station the following day, and told their story to a patient officer, one they both suspected from her manner was probably inured to the never-ending dangers of petty domestic disputes. They did get assurances that the matter would be investigated. They never heard if it had been.

*

Lucy didn't know of the second meeting Ed had with Craig the day after they'd been to the police, and he didn't tell her. Craig had discovered a legal solution in his favour would be unlikely, and he was in no position to pay the lawyer's fees. There was no guarantee, even if he did win, that he would be awarded costs. So he decided his only choice was the brotherly love approach. At first he'd detected a softening in Ed's reaction at the meeting, and decided to appeal to his better nature.

His plan was to intercept Ed on the street, making sure Lucy was not with him. She was the real enemy, his nemesis. The way she'd looked at him! Bitch! He didn't have to wait for long. Ed's movements to and from work were predictable.

'Hello, Ed,' he said cheerily, as if their meeting was a surprise, and they had parted the best of friends. 'I'm sorry that things didn't end too well the other day. I think I must have come across as rather demanding. Sorry.'

Ed was instantly on guard, determined not to give Craig a way in. 'Demanding! You certainly were that,' Ed replied.

'I just felt,' Craig answered, 'that Dad may have left some provision for me. But of course if you say he didn't…'

'He didn't, Craig, and with his death, the house became my mothers. I believe it was in both their names.' He could see where Craig was taking this, abandoning the legal claim because it had no legs, and making what he considered to be a moral one, an appeal to fairness. And Ed would have none of it.

'I thought as a brother, you might…' Craig was fighting to remain reasonable, and becoming increasingly angry as he sensed he was losing the battle almost before it had begun. He'd planned to mention his proposed engagement to Fern, and his struggle to make ends meet, to salvage his life as Ed had done, but he didn't get the chance.

'I'm in a hurry, Craig. I've discussed it with my wife,' Ed interrupted, wanting to end the exchange. 'And she agrees with me that…'

His bloody wife again, Craig cursed silently. The meeting was effectively over.

*

It was the call from the nursing home he knew would come, and come soon. But even something expected can be a shock when it crosses the divide from abstract to the real.

'You'd better come quickly,' a gentle female voice said, and then as if anticipating his question, 'Not very long now, Mr Grainger.'

Lucy offered to come with him, but he felt he had to do this alone. It was an intimacy he needed. Lucy had felt the same when entrusted to look after her father's affairs. Besides, his mother had never really known Lucy.

'Don't wait up,' he told her. 'I don't know how long…'

He was greeted caringly at the door by a nurse who assured him his mother was comfortable, and walked with him to her room, gently closing the door behind him.

She lay supine on the bed, her mouth open, unhinged, eyes closed, her face lucent and slightly grey. Her hair had been neatly combed but looked sparse like maidenhair.

One of the nurses must have put some white roses in a small vase on her bedside table. On the other was a framed photo of their small family in the early days, his father beaming and towering over them all, Todd with a silly grin, he looking shy, and his prideful mother. The rest of the room was bare except for a grey metal wardrobe, a small writing desk, and a familiar Manet print on the wall.

So this was where it was to end for her. He remembered reading the story of Robin Hood as a child, and how Robin, sitting up in his sickbed, had enough strength to shoot an arrow from the window, saying he wanted to be buried where the arrow landed. How many of us ever get the choice of where to die?

Ed had heard that the comatose can hear your every word. Nurses tell you to profess your love, tell them you'll be fine when they go, seek absolution if you need it, and if you're so inclined, then pray.

He spoke to her, sitting on a bedside chair, and leaning close so that she might hear. He told her what a wonderful mother she had been,

96

but if she thought her time had come…and he didn't know how to frame the rest. She would understand.

Life had not been kind to her in recent years, and he didn't want her to endure it any longer if it was all too much, certainly not for his sake. Sometimes he was light-hearted and laughed. At other times he was anguished and had to battle to stop the flow of tears.

The nursing staff brought him a cup of tea and a sandwich, and waived nursing home policy by making him a makeshift couch in her room so they could spend the night together. Lucy would understand. As it became darker, there was a pervasive silence and he could see shadows flickering beyond the window. He'd watch the calmness of her face, and listen to her stertorous breath rasp life from laden air.

He didn't sleep. His endless chatter to her revived odd images, her raiding the box of Turkish delight and strenuously denying it, laughing as she did so, the way she'd bite her lip when curious or absorbed, the funny way she'd throw a ball when they played catchings on the beach, her gambolling about when excited, and the endless tokens and novel ways she'd invent of expressing her love. All so long ago.

At two thirty a.m. the grating sound stopped, and a palpable stillness filled the room. For a few seconds, he wondered if she was enjoying a more comfortable sleep, but he soon realised it was an eternal sleep.

Whenever people later spoke of the spirit moving, this was the moment he'd remember. He knew there was no need to press buzzers or call for help. There was no hurry. For years, he'd try to recall the exact nature of his feelings at that moment. There was shock, even though he'd been prepared for it, and with the numbness there was a profound emptiness.

She was at peace now, and he didn't want to leave her. These were precious moments as she prepared for a final journey. He was resentful of being disturbed, not wanting the intrusion of an indifferent world.

It must have been two hours later that he kissed her one final time and, after lingering at the door, still reluctant to leave, approached the nurses' station to find a single nurse on duty. He didn't say a word. One look and she knew. She went to his mother to confirm, and returned to nod. She very gently explained the procedure the nursing home would follow, and escorted him to the front doors, placing a hand on his arm as a gesture of sympathy.

'I'm so sorry, Mr Grainger, but she's at peace now. She was a lovely woman, often spoke about you, never one bit of trouble,' she said, and Ed thought that was a fitting epitaph. She never had been any trouble.

His drive away was metaphor, consigning present loss to mellow past, advancing by retreat. The world was still asleep, the darkness of the streets blushed by amber stars, and his mother was everywhere, the brief ubiquity that's granted when you kiss the cheek of time.

'Don't leave me,' he said aloud. 'Not yet.'

As the car moved noiselessly on empty roads, their dialogue was loving and pure, and while he was sore at heart, they were at peace, not raging against the dying of the light.

8

'They're the only ones we know of who might have had a reason,' Ken said uncertainly.

Clive turned to look at the whiteboard where Ken had written the names, and scribbled notes underneath. 'Of course it mightn't be any of them.'

'You said at the beginning you didn't think it was a burglary gone wrong,' Kane commented, more assured now after a few months of police work and the support from his superiors. 'Do you still think that?'

'Without a doubt,' Clive answered. 'It all points to someone who knew her. We have suspects, though that's too strong a word for some of them. We have persons of interest. But do we have the right one? There might be any number of people out there who held a grudge.'

'It's been a while without any answers,' Ken offered.

'Don't remind me. The big boys in the city are pressuring me, wanting an answer, like yesterday,' Clive replied, yet not looking particularly disturbed.

'Are they going to give us any more resources?' Kane asked.

'They've promised half a dozen men for three days,' Clive answered. 'Called it a task force. Ken, can I leave that with you? We'll talk about it later. For now, we've all been at the interviews, so let's go through our so-called suspects one at a time, perhaps starting with the least likely.'

He put his feet up on the desk. He seemed to do most of his thinking in that position. His colleagues joked about it. Ken sat upright in view of the whiteboard. It was his preferred modus operandi. Kane was restless, moving from chair to chair. He was enjoying the intrigue of criminal investigation, and was grateful to Clive for his involvement.

'Anne Keating,' Clive began, 'mid-forties, work colleague of Lucy's. Ken?'

'Was beaten for promotion by Lucy who'd only been with the company for a few months when she'd been there for several years. Thought the job was hers. She was so worked up about it she tried to play a really hurtful trick on Lucy, one meant to make her lose her job altogether, but apart from hurting Lucy, it embarrassed the boss, and she was fired.'

'Almost classic,' Kane interrupted. 'She causes personal injury, and then blames the completely innocent person who made her angry enough to do so.'

'Anyway,' Ken resumed, 'she made threats.' He looked at his notes and read, '"you haven't heard the end of this". Said it in front of the whole staff.'

'Doc said the murderer needed considerable strength to inflict the wound,' Clive was exploring all the options. 'Do you think…'

'You saw her, Clive. She's built like a tank,' Kane anticipated. 'She'd be as strong as a lot of men.'

'And at interview?'

'Very subdued,' Ken commented. 'Said she was sorry about Lucy. We didn't believe her for a moment, and she couldn't help saying that she should have got the promotion. Couldn't help herself. You'd think under the circumstances… Obvious she's still nursing her grievance.'

'Alibi?' Clive asked.

'You must remember her saying she was at Buckingham Palace the night it happened, having scones with the Queen. When told it was no laughing matter, said she's home every night with the family, cooking and cleaning up after two ungrateful kids, except for art classes on Fridays. But it wouldn't have been hard for her to get to the Graingers's between eight and nine. They live nearby, and she says they eat early, and do their own thing most of the time.'

'What do we think?'

'Wouldn't want to get on the wrong side of her, but work disputes like this are a dime a dozen. Happens every day in a thousand places,'

Ken said. 'People make threats, swear they're going to kill someone, and the next day it's as if it never happened. It's all blown over. I don't think she's our murderer.'

'I agree,' Kane added hesitantly. 'But she was one of the angriest people I've come across, and it hadn't blown over, not just with Lucy, but with the whole world. She thought life had cheated her. All that anger building up, festering… Might Lucy have been a trigger, the final straw…'

'Not likely then, but not out of the frame entirely. Daniel Westerly, twenty-seven, ex-fiancé. Kane, what's your take on Daniel?'

'They were engaged and Lucy went overseas to her sister's place to clear her head because she had doubts about the marriage, away for four months, and when she came back, she dropped him immediately. He was furious, believed she knew all the time, and was just stringing him along. He'd been pining, fixing up the place. We don't know any details of how it ended or what he said, whether he threatened her or not. All we know came from a friend of his. At interview, Westerly said he was very angry, but didn't threaten her. Said it wasn't like him to do so. He was stunned to hear of Lucy's death, and was emotional when he asked for details about it.'

'Yes, he was.' Ken took over. 'But we shouldn't be mislead by that. It wouldn't be the first time a murderer wept over his victim. Everyone thinks that an outward show of grief and a fountain of tears is proof of integrity.'

'And there was something about a job, remember,' Kane recalled. 'Once in a lifetime opportunity… She didn't want him to take it. He didn't say much about it, possibly because he didn't want to show he was angry. Better to show he still cared than to show anger. But I got the impression he'd have taken the job if he'd been aware of Lucy's real feelings for him.'

'So he has more than one reason to be filthy with Lucy,' Ken commented.

There was silence for a few seconds before Clive spoke.

'You know the saying, "hell hath no fury like a woman scorned", but what about a man scorned? Is it any different? Might his rejection have been eating at him for many months until the sore had to break out?'

'That's the very reason I don't put him high on my list of suspects.' Kane picked up the thread. 'Surely if he wanted to do her real harm, he wouldn't have waited this long to do so. We spoke to some of his acquaintances, and they all said he wasn't an aggressive sort of bloke.'

'But even the most mild-mannered little old lady is capable of terrible deeds if she's been abused, or she's missed the chance of a lifetime. You spoke about his rejection festering, Clive,' Ken resumed. 'Perhaps it just needed a trigger, and what more effective trigger could there be than Lucy marrying another man, and so soon after she's given him his marching orders? Might he not see that as a double insult…throw him over in favour of someone else. I said double. It might be triple. He might even have believed that the someone else had always been there.'

'I think that would hurt each of us,' Clive summed up. 'Kane, if your Sarah said it was all over between you, and was married to someone else several months later…' He stopped, realising the analogy wasn't appropriate.

'I'm not a violent man,' Kane started to answer, 'but I'd be tempted…'

'So what do we think… Kane?'

'I think if he was going to act, he would have done it earlier.'

'Ken?'

'I'm not so sure. I'm not prepared to rule him out just yet.'

'Very wise,' Clive concluded.

'Adrian Passmore, early forties, married, two children in posh schools, highly successful lawyer. Ken?'

'Not really a suspect at all. More a person of interest. He was a professional acquaintance. Lucy approached him to help work out everything with her deceased father's estate and business affairs. Perfectly innocent, except we got an anonymous phone call saying he'd been seen with Lucy outside business hours. We got the phone records and traced the call to a Blanche Louvier. Turned out to be his private secretary.'

'We interviewed her,' Kane continued the story, 'and she was really tight-lipped, scared as all hell, didn't have anything more to tell us, only that she had seen them meeting after the normal end of business at five thirty. Didn't want to say where. Was scared about losing her job. Wanted us to swear we wouldn't tell him about the phone call or the interview.'

'Why do you think she made the call, Kane?'

'Ken thinks she was hostile with her boss,' and he nodded towards Ken. 'I think it was jealousy. And we both have doubts about her reliability. She did admit to getting help for mental instability. What was it, Ken?'

'Anxiety disorder. In the interview, she was restless, couldn't concentrate.'

'Perhaps that's what I've got,' Kane laughed.

The others didn't.

'Thing is,' Ken resumed, 'there's no real evidence of any impropriety, and except for one call from a person with highly suspect motives, no reason to think there was anything between Lucy and Passmore. He might have liked her, they might have liked each other, but if you want to put him on the list of suspects, we'd better check out the baker, the grocer, the butcher and candlestick maker.'

'And what did he have to gain?' Kane added. 'Even if there was something more than friendship, there's no motive. A glamorous wife, two kids at posh schools. And he certainly had a lot to lose. If he'd wanted a bit more action, I reckon this Louvier woman would have been prepared to oblige.'

'Could she have…?' Ken was thinking aloud, and decided not to go further.

'I don't think so.' Clive read his thoughts. 'Doesn't quite fit with the anxiety disorder. So both nos?' Clive looked at his colleagues.

They both nodded, Kane more slowly.

'He was certainly shaken at interview when we told him a little about the murder.' Clive still had his feet on the desk.

'Berice Downing, early thirties, no fixed employment, unskilled part-time work. Kane?'

'Mad as a meat axe.'

'It's a hard one to figure,' Ken interrupted, 'for that very reason. She'd be capable of anything, however bizarre.'

'And the strength factor?' Clive asked.

'Not built like Anne Keating. Mad as she might be, I can't see it,' Ken answered.

'I can,' Kane said. 'People are capable of anything when they get themselves into a rage. She'd surely have the best motive of them all. Look at all the letters. All the protests of love. What about the argument she had with Lucy when she was caught at the letter box, telling her she wasn't as good-looking as she thought she'd be, and finding out Lucy had read her letters and thought them a joke?'

'But she's mad, Kane,' Ken interjected, 'a sicko.'

'Might be, but doesn't that make it more likely rather than less likely, that she could do something crazy? A good number of our murderers are out of their minds with a cocktail of alcohol and ice. With Lucy out of the way, she'd think she could have Ed to herself. You saw her at the interview, not a shred of remorse or sympathy over Lucy's death. Her eyes lit up.'

'And that worries me,' Ken countered. 'You'd think the murderer wouldn't be as transparently pleased. Wouldn't they try to hide their pleasure?'

'But you've already said she's mad.'

Something was troubling Ken. They didn't agree on this one.

'Whether mad or not,' he said quietly, 'I don't think she's very bright. Could she have left the crime scene without leaving any clues? The murderer made a real effort to remove incriminating evidence. Is that Berice? Wouldn't it be more likely that she'd rush away covered in blood and brandishing a bloodied knife, and go straight to Ed to tell him the way was now clear for them both?'

'Bit cynical isn't it, Ken?' Clive commented. 'All right, we don't agree on that one.' He wasn't giving his own opinion, and he wasn't adjudicating.

'Derek Downing, mid-thirties, metalworker, husband of Berice. Ken?'

'I think we'll agree on this one. No question of not being strong enough. A powerful man with a reputation for being a brawler, loves a fight. A problem with anger, and he was furious, beside himself with rage after assaulting Ed and being charged with assault by the Chatswood boys.'

'And at our interview,' Kane added, 'when asked about Lucy's death, he said "So" just like that. A belligerent so, and looked at us defiantly. Couldn't give a damn. No real alibi, except being home with his wife the night it happened. She'd said they did their own thing after dinner, and of course they'd alibi each other.'

'Apart from his disagreement with Ed,' Ken resumed, 'he had the best motive of all. He'd been convinced one way or another by Berice, whether she really believed it, or she was playing games, that Ed was trying to take her away from him. And she was his world, the poor bugger, so in his own twisted way, he thought he'd retaliate by taking Lucy away from Ed.'

'He was incensed enough with what he thought Ed was doing, but two other things tipped him over the edge,' Kane continued. 'One was being charged with assault, and the other was his own wife openly admitting that she was in love with Ed.'

'He has to be the prime suspect,' Ken said. 'Ed supposedly pursuing his wife, his wife admitting her love for Ed, the charge of assault…even his hatred fed by Ed refusing to get up and fight like a man.'

'But Ken, what of your point about the lack of evidence at the crime scene? Derek isn't even as bright as Berice. If she might rush out – what did you say, brandishing a bloodied knife? – Derek would probably put it on Facebook.'

'He could have crept in, killed her and crept back out without leaving evidence.'

'Does that mean you've changed your mind about Berice?' Clive asked.

Ken saw the contradiction, but shook his head without answering.

'A prime suspect for you too, Kane?' Clive asked.

'Certainly one of two.'

'Finally, Craig Granger, eighteen or nineteen, no birth certificate, itinerant labourer and surprise half-brother of Ed. Who wants to start?'

'I will,' Ken said. 'Arrived to announce himself as Ed's half-brother, which came as a complete surprise to the Graingers, and to report on his, or their, father's death in Rockhampton. Assumed that hearing about both would swamp Ed with brotherly love, or guilt, or sympathy, and that he would be an easy target. Cocky little bugger. But when he put the hard word on them about his rightful claim to some inheritance or cash, he was rejected, and they told him to get out.'

'The significant thing here,' Kane took over, a little to Ken's annoyance, 'was that Lucy was the more hostile of the two. Apparently, Ed tried to reason with him, and was possibly a little sympathetic, but Lucy could see from the start what he was angling for, took an instant dislike to him, and didn't mind him seeing it. She was the one who pushed Ed to report his threats to the police.' Kane looked at his notes. 'He said, "Make no mistake, you'll regret this."'

'The Chatswood boys said he was furious when they finally tracked him down and paid him a visit. They did a check and found he has a record of assault in Rockhampton and Townsville.'

'Alibi?'

'No, but he hasn't got to know many people here yet to alibi him. He's staying in a youth hostel. Says he was probably out drinking. Gave us the name of several pubs, but can't remember which ones and at what times. Said it might have been all of them. We sent some uniforms to ask at the named ones, but no one could remember him.'

'He has no history of permanent employment. Then again, he is only eighteen or nineteen. Desperate for money.'

'And there's supposed to be a girl back home who wants to make an honest man out of him. He's supposed to be really keen on her. Might explain the sudden need of cash.'

'So what's the motive?' Clive asked. 'Does he think that with Lucy out of the way, he'd have a better chance of twisting Ed's arm?'

'Either that,' Ken answered, 'or simple hate of Lucy.'

'Hate is never simple,' Clive smiled. 'So you both have Craig up there with Derek?'

They both nodded.

'Ken, the task force of half a dozen men we were promised will arrive on Wednesday, eight a.m. sharp. I think we need to talk again not just to the neighbours, but do a wider door-knock of the neighbourhood. We need help running checks on the suspects, and scouring the area, bushland, ponds, dumpsters. That knife has to be somewhere. Ed's not in the house now, so it would help to have some fresh eyes to look there again. Can I leave you to coordinate that?'

Ken was pleased. It was the meticulous planning he was good at. And if he were to be successful...

'I'll be there at the briefing on Wednesday morning, but I'll leave you to run it.'

'Clive,' Kane asked, 'you've heard what we think, but you haven't told us what you think.'

For the first time in their meeting, Clive removed his feet from his desk and sat looking vacantly out the window. 'I really don't know what to think,' he answered.

'Don't you believe it, Kane,' Ken said, and winked.

9

Ed returned once to his house a few days after the murder to collect a few changes of clothes and toiletries. The first days were spent with Lois and Ted Channing who, having conferred him with celebrity status, wanted to show him off to their friends and were disappointed to see him leave.

He went to the nearby house of a friend who was leaving for overseas, where he could never shake the feeling of being alone in a strange world. It was like blundering around in someone else's very personal milieu. Would things ever be the same for him again? He slept in a strange bed, found it difficult to get the right temperature in the shower, had to search for washing-up liquid, and learn when and how the garbage was collected. He rarely ventured outside, and didn't answer the door.

The media frenzy subsided after a few days, and although his whereabouts were unknown, he found the silence oppressive rather than welcoming. He wanted peace and quiet. He needed peace and quiet, but the house was heavy and palpable with stillness and foreboding.

It was a large four-bedroom house with a spacious back veranda, and a pool, but Ed confined himself to the main bedroom, en suite and kitchen. To roam further was a threat, a challenge to learn a further set of particularities.

He knew he was depressed, and he thought sleep was a salve for depression. It was supposed to shut out painful thoughts. He'd lie down shortly after his very basic evening meal of macaroni and cheese, but sleep often eluded him, and when it did come, the dreams were not always pleasant.

He had one disturbing and recurring dream. He was a school-age boy standing before a man who was furious with him, abusing him for something he'd done, but he didn't know what it was. He stood with his hands by his sides, and his head down, shamed and ashamed. Every so often, he would look up and the man would not be there. It would be someone else taking his place, an endless gallery of detractors intent on his censure, an old woman, a young boy, a teenage girl, a cleric, doctor, council worker, all accusing him. And he'd look different too, a boy, an adolescent, an adult, an old man, but all of them him.

Fleetingly, his mother's face would appear in front of him, superimposed on whoever was tearing strips off him at the time. 'I love you,' she'd say.

And always one of his accusers was a skull, its muddy teeth hideously conspicuous, fixed in a bony jaw. It too would be full of accusation, its mandible clicking open and shut, its hollow eyes, or large orbs where eyes used to be, staring at him.

The scene would suddenly switch to his mother, grey, disconcertingly still on her deathbed.

When he wasn't dreaming, he'd recreate the images that gave him pleasure, standing in line in front of Lucy when they were voting at the federal elections, their nonsense exchange of words, and the excitement of a connection between them he knew even then was special. And he relived their weekend away, fleeing the teeth of the storm to Mrs Willoughby's guest house, the look Lucy gave him, as she emerged towelled from the bath, hot and scented, and the magic of what followed.

There was room too in his imaginings for his early days. The eagerly anticipated Sunday outings in the old Ford Prefect with the sweet smell of his mother's lavender and chocolate. The morning and afternoon teas she'd bring to the intrepid infant explorers in their spaceship submarine. The improvised bedtime radio serials with Todd. Those first idyllic days at Forster.

They were precious memories, but he'd often drift into sleep and wake up more depressed. They were ancient memories blurring in the amnesia of history. Nothing more. They were not enough to sustain him. The realities could never be repeated.

Lucy, his mother, his father, Todd, all gone. All of them too young. What right did he have to live on? Who made that choice, and what did it signify? Was it for him a blessing or a punishment?

*

'Guilty! He's bloody guilty! Lois! Lois!' Ted Channing, now on his feet, yelled. 'Get in here quick. It's on the TV. Grainger! Grainger's guilty! He's the murderer!'

'I don't believe it.' Lois rushed into the family room carrying a tea towel and sat down heavily next to Ted, who turned up the volume.

The six o'clock evening news on Channel Nine had begun with a newsflash. An account of the floods in Western Australia was interrupted. 'News has just been received from police headquarters,' a poker-faced newsreader began, 'that Ed Grainger, the husband of Mrs Lucy Grainger, a respected business woman and well-known social identity from the North Shore of Sydney, who was found brutally murdered in their Turramurra home a month ago, has confessed to her murder. The investigation, led by Inspector Clive Jeffries, unearthed critical evidence that proves beyond a doubt…'

'He's guilty!' The word was growing in stature for Ted as he kept repeating it like a mantra, as if it was battling to imprint itself on a sluggish brain. 'Guilty'. The word wasn't large enough to contain an awful truth. He kept standing and sitting, standing and sitting. 'He's confessed.'

'Sshhh.' Lois didn't want to miss a word. 'Listen!'

'It is understood that Grainger, who the day after the murder made an impassioned plea to the public for their help, is assisting police with their enquiries.'

It was the first news item, and lasted for several minutes. It reported on Ed finally confessing when faced with the weight of evidence against him. The detail of that evidence could not be revealed for legal reasons. It showed a fifteen-second snippet of Clive Jeffries and Ken Carpenter sitting with him across a table in the interview room, followed by a press interview with Ken Carpenter saying with ill-disguised hubris, 'It was sound, methodical police work. Yes, he's guilty all right. The evidence is incontrovertible.'

Parts of Ed's first interview after the murder, containing his matter-of-fact profession of love for Lucy were shown, as was the earlier glamorous photograph of Lucy. Even the house was pictured.

Lois and Ted watched, riveted to the screen.

'Good Lord.' Lois, who'd moved closer to the television to better see the pictures of Ed, sat down heavily when the floods in Western Australia were reintroduced, and remained speechless while the prime minister appeared to talk about the economy. 'Just think, we had a murderer living with us,' she eventually said. 'I hugged him the very night he did it, fresh from murdering Lucy, blood on his hands, invited him into our home. He sat at the same dinner table, slept in the next room.' She was becoming more agitated. 'And poor Honey. What did that poor dog think was going on when he was…when he…?' She stifled a sob.

Her mind was racing. She'd had another thought. 'Ted, he might have attacked me during the night. He might have killed us both while we were sleeping.'

'Ed Grainger. Of all the people, gentle Ed Grainger. Certainly had us fooled,' Ted replied. 'I never would have thought…didn't seem that sort of bloke…but when you think about it…still waters run deep.'

'I have to ring Stacey and Julie…and Peta of course.' Lois didn't wait for Ted's thoughts, and she rushed to the phone with an absorbing evening ahead. A newspaper account, 'A Killer in My Home', wasn't beyond the bounds of possibility. Or 'His Bloodied Arms Held Me'. She'd enjoyed the media attention after the murder, but now…

The story remained the lead item for the next two nights on the television news, usurping the accounts of the tsunami in Indonesia that killed thousands, the failure of international climate change initiatives in a European court, the public disgrace of a British royal, the assassination of an influential leader in a South American country, and the American president's most recent gaffe.

The press had a field day. One newspaper carried the headline 'Great Acting Before the Final Curtain'. Another in huge lettering simply said, 'Hypocrite', displayed an unflattering photo of Ed, and presented the sketchy details of his upbringing, suggesting links to future deviant behaviour.

The public reaction was hostile. Most people had been convinced by Ed's genuineness, so his deception was doubly hurtful. They felt he had made fools of them. 'He seemed such a nice man,' was a common reaction of many female viewers.

Of course there were many who had the gift of hindsight and boasted to their partners that they had known all along. 'How often do we see it,' they'd crow, 'the grief and protests of love as proof of probity to convince a gullible public.' Some of them argued that in time, a person's fiction could become their truth, until they started to believe in their own innocence. That might well be Ed Grainger.

The report galvanised women who'd been protesting about domestic violence, and two days after the news, they marched in Sydney, Adelaide and Melbourne, causing traffic mayhem. The placards reporting that one woman was killed, a victim of domestic violence, every day in Australia, kept the story of Lucy's murder alive. Some carried pictures of Lucy.

The newspapers and radio shock jocks criticised the politicians for not doing enough to address the problem. The relevant government ministers briefly lost their smugness, defending their position by relating what government initiatives had been put in place. The usual masterful dodging. Some foreshadowed sweeping new measures to combat the problem. A few called for a reintroduction of the death penalty.

'The house will go for a song,' the local estate agents agreed.

*

Ken Carpenter had reason to be pleased. He'd followed Clive's suggestions in coordinating the work of the task force. Every house within hundreds of metres of the murder scene had been door-knocked, the area was combed for physical evidence, and one member, a computer buff, had been given the task of finding what he could dredge up about the suspects or persons of interest. The pieces had fallen into place.

The door knock yielded no result but must have prompted the anonymous phone call to the police. It was a male voice reporting seeing a man surreptitiously throwing something wrapped in a rag into a local pond, a few streets from where Ed had lived. The caller couldn't be sure of the man's identity, as it was twilight, he was new to the area and some distance away. Yes, it was the right size to be a knife. He gave a brief and vague description of the man.

'So what was the description?' a calm Ken Carpenter asked.

He wasn't excited. There were always calls like these from oddballs wanting to make mischief, who thrived on watching the activity they created. There'd already been two others. But the description the anonymous caller gave matched that of Ed Grainger. No need to get too excited, though, because the description was sketchy, and there was nothing particularly distinctive about Ed.

'Where is this pond?' the task force officer taking the call asked. He was an officer from another area command and didn't know, but wanted to keep the caller talking.

It didn't work. The phone went dead, and they had no luck tracing the call.

They were lucky. There was only one pond. It was a brackish pool of water roughly forty metres in diameter in an overgrown park three hundred metres from Ed's house. Water lilies covered one corner, and a few large tree branches floated on the surface attracting scum. The park was overgrown and surrounded by bush, so parents didn't like their children playing there. It was, though, a favourite place for couples wanting privacy.

Ken was uncertain what to do. Sending divers there would be a significant use of his limited resources. He asked Clive's advice, and they interviewed the officer who'd taken the call.

'A little nervy,' Officer Sweet answered them, 'but yeah, genuine, I think, but how do you know? They'd be nervy if it was just a crank call too…afraid of being caught.'

'But your overall impression, Sweet?' Ken pushed. 'This is really important.'

Officer Sweet knew the likely outcome of restating his belief that the caller was genuine, but he stood his ground. 'I think he was genuine, but I could be wrong.'

'What did you make of him, Clive?' Ken asked when Officer Sweet had gone. He had great faith in his boss's intuition.

'As the man said, he could be wrong,' Clive answered, 'but I'm inclined to trust his judgement. I liked him. But I wonder why the caller didn't want to identify himself.'

'Didn't want to get involved, I suppose,' Ken replied. 'Might mean going to court, reprisals if there wasn't a conviction.'

After discussing the risk with Clive, Ken took a chance and ordered a search of the pond. Clive was able to twist the arms at headquarters and secure two specialist divers. They arrived early in the morning and set to work. It hadn't rained for over a week, so the water wasn't as muddy as it might have been.

Ken waited patiently all morning, and when there'd been no news, feeling dejected, went to the pond site to see for himself. 'Nothing?' he queried.

That was obvious.

'It's filthy down there,' one of the divers replied, 'silt, leaves, rubbish. We have to clear away, and dig down as we go, do a little at a time. Look,' and he pointed to a pile on the pond's edge, a pile of old working boots, a rusted lamp, wooden shelving, wall brackets, and what looked like engine parts. 'Another few hours, but not looking good.'

It rained late in the afternoon and the search was abandoned.

A dispirited Ken Carpenter returned to the office to report to Clive. 'Perhaps Sweet was wrong,' he said.

'Possibly not,' answered Clive, with his feet on the desk. 'We have the divers for another day. There's still hope. Where were they searching?'

'Every centimetre of the pond. Why?'

'If you were trying to make sure the murder weapon wasn't found, where would you throw it?' Clive asked.

'In the middle.'

Ken joined the searchers for the day, and when they'd finished, shaking their heads, he asked them to look again in the middle of the pond. He sat on a fallen tree and waited. Things hadn't worked out as he'd hoped. He needed to think of another plan, but what?

Late in the afternoon, they found the knife, still wrapped in a rag and tied with string. Ken was still there when one of the divers surfaced holding the prize aloft.

'It would have to be where we'd already looked,' he said. 'But it's hard to see anything down there.'

Ken wasn't the demonstrative type, but it was difficult to conceal his delight when the rag was carefully unwrapped.

The knife was subjected to close forensic examination, but there were no traces of blood to match it to Lucy's blood type. Doc said he couldn't swear to it, but it was certainly consistent with the weapon that had inflicted Lucy's fatal injury.

While badly smudged, there were sufficient fingerprints on the knife to identify a killer. Ken was hopeful. There needed to be a record of the murderer's prints, and the police didn't have records for the majority of people. Still, they would run the prints through their database.

One of the task force members assigned to examine the murder scene reported that the knife found in the pond was probably one of a set of knives in Ed's house. The knives were the same except they were all of varying sizes. So it was quickly established that the murderer hadn't brought his or her own knife. A house knife had been used.

'Doesn't look as if it was premeditated,' Ken reported. 'The killer must have grabbed the knife when disturbed or in a rage.'

'Clive might be wrong,' Kane said to Ken confidentially. 'It might well have been a burglary gone wrong.'

The world of the three chief investigators was turned on its head the following day when Ken rushed into the main office breathing heavily. Clive and Kane were sitting quietly at their desks.

'You're not going to believe this,' he panted. 'The fingerprints, we did have them on record, guess who, just heard. Ed Grainger's. Can you believe it?'

Kane was dumbfounded. Clive was startled. Ken was excited.

'I just can't believe,' Clive said softly, 'that I could have been that wrong about Ed.'

'Pick him up, Clive?' Ken asked.

'Let's not get ahead of ourselves,' Clive answered, always the voice of moderation. 'Ed might have used the knife to cut up vegetables. The killer might have worn gloves when he used the same knife. Of course that doesn't explain why the knife ended up in the pond. But I still think we need more.'

Ken was disappointed. He didn't agree. He'd have arrested Ed immediately, but Clive was the senior officer, and he knew better than to argue. But how could the fact that Ed's fingerprints were on the knife, and no one else's, be explained. There was only one explanation. Ed would hardly have chopped up vegetables with his wife lying dead on the floor. And then there was the description, not just of how the man looked, but the distinctive way he walked. Ed Grainger!

The same day, another idea occurred to Ken that was all his own. He remembered Doc saying when they were inspecting the body that, given the wound, the murderer's clothes would probably be blood-spattered. That had been confirmed by the coroner. The house had been thoroughly searched, as had dumpsters and local bushland. No bloodied clothing had been found. No shirts, blouses or dresses had been salvaged from the pond.

It was a long shot because the killer would probably have disposed of a bloodied shirt rather than try to restore it for normal wear. The natural thing to do would be to cut it into small fragments and dispose of each in a different place. Or burn it.

Better to explore all options. He ordered an internet search of every dry cleaner within a radius of twenty kilometres, and asked the task force members to visit each one. He'd start with twenty kilometres, and decide about ranging further afield later. The killer would be foolish to go to the nearest cleaners, but probably wouldn't expect such a search to take place. There was a chance that one of the cleaners might remember a bloodied shirt, blouse or dress given for cleaning a few weeks before.

Each team was allocated several dry cleaners, and set about their work the following day. Ken and Kane sat impatiently in the office waiting.

The first two teams returned with no result. 'A few little drops of blood on the collar of a shirt, no doubt nicks from shaving,' one of the team members reported. 'That was the closest we got.'

The last visiting team of investigators to report back brought the damning news. They questioned the owner of a small dry cleaners eighteen kilometres away.

'Sure, I remember,' he said. 'We don't often get a shirt spattered in that much blood. Had to wonder what sort of injury the poor bloke suffered. What happened to you, I said…run into a chainsaw? He said nothing, smiled, I think…looked all right, though.'

The task force members were instantly alert, and produced a photo of Ed.

'Yeah, that's him. Hey, come to think of it, isn't that the bloke… Thought I'd seen him before.'

'Do you have any record of the job?' The investigators asked.

'Sure, I do,' and the dry cleaner, proud of his efficiency, and what he suspected to be his new status in possibly helping to solve a murder, went to a system of cards revealing Ed's name, the job date, job item and his signature.

'Surprising, isn't it,' he called after the excited and quickly retreating investigators, 'how people become so attached to a favourite piece of clothing. If it had been mine…'

There could be little doubt now, particularly as none of the other sixteen dry cleaners had any record of cleaning anything owned by a

Mr Grainger, or anything with more than the smallest spot of blood. And if Ed had wanted something cleaned, why did he travel eighteen kilometres, and bypass at least a dozen other dry cleaners to do so?

*

Clive accompanied Ken to make the arrest. He did so with a heavy heart. He thought it a shame because there was residual pity for Ed, and he liked the man, but he also remembered what must have been a consummately acted show of both alarm and grief the night he met him, standing with him beyond the cordoned-off area while he innocently asked what had happened, and when he was told, wanting to know if she'd been interfered with sexually. He'd been so convincing. But worst of all was his asking if he could see Lucy. Why? To look ghoulishly at his own handiwork? And later, at the media interview, what seemed to be his impressive struggle to control his pain. He'd found Ed's lack of overt anguish convincing too. It might explain why he didn't want to say much, wanted Clive to make the appeals to the public. He was annoyed. Very annoyed. He wasn't often fooled.

Of course, he also reasoned that Ed was probably genuinely distraught at having committed a murder, and that would have explained his reaction when he arrived back at the crime scene. He may have been disoriented, battling to come to grips with it, or even believe what he'd done. It may have been one insane moment that could never be reclaimed. It was after all a single knife wound and not frenzied repetitions. He may have genuinely loved her, might have lashed out, not ever intending to kill her.

Kane, the first to meet Ed at the murder scene, was also surprised, and felt a younger man's intolerance of being duped. As an inexperienced officer, he felt his greenness had been exploited by Ed's frantic, halting questions seeking clarity for what he already knew. Like Clive, he could understand Ed's emotional reaction. That was easy to explain, even his being sick in the gutter. After all, it wasn't every day you committed a murder.

'You need to come with us, Ed,' Clive said stonily. 'I don't think you need me to tell you why.'

Ed showed no resistance or defiance accompanying them to the police station. There was no need for handcuffs. He seemed defeated when presented with the evidence, and wasn't very forthcoming in the interview conducted by Clive and Ken with Kane as observer.

'We have the evidence, Mr Grainger,' Ken began.

An interview of this nature demanded formality. Ken and Clive sat on one side of the table, and Ed on the other with his hands palm down on the table. The interview room had no other furniture except for a single chair that Kane sat on.

Ken was raring to begin. He didn't share Clive's liking of Ed. Thought him altogether a slippery character. 'Let's start with the knife. We know it was the murder weapon, and it has your prints on it…and no one else's. How can you explain that?'

Ed shrugged. 'There's six in the set,' he said, slowly and barely audibly. 'I use them for cutting meat and vegetables.'

Clive was watching him intently.

'You don't think it's strange that there were no other prints, only yours?'

'Perhaps the killer wiped…' He stopped, shrugged again, but gave no answer.

'All right,' Ken continued, 'why would we find a knife with your prints on it in a pond? If yours are the only prints, and it was the murder weapon, why would anyone else want to get rid of the knife?'

Again Ed gave no answer. Only a slight shake of the head.

'You were seen going to the pond, and throwing something in.' The witness had described a man that might have been Ed, but Ken wanted to see how Ed reacted.

Clive frowned.

Again, no response from Ed.

'Then there's the matter of the shirt.' This was Ken's coup. 'Covered in blood and your name and date on the dry cleaner's docket. And it's a Ganton, the same, except for the colour, as several of your other shirts. How do you explain that? Do you deny taking it to the cleaners?'

'I don't know,' Ed answered softly.

Kane was wishing he could become more involved, but knew that wouldn't be welcomed. It was meant to be a learning experience. He knew what to ask!

'Ed,' Clive took over, 'can you tell us why you took your shirt, whatever had made it all bloody, to a dry cleaner's so far away? There were sixteen dry cleaners closer.'

They waited for an answer.

'I guess I must have been in the area at the time.'

'You guess? Surely you'd remember if you were there for something else.'

There was no answer. Only a shrug.

Ken looked across at Clive and shook his head in frustration. Ed wasn't exactly being uncooperative, but he wasn't likely to reveal much. He was sitting languidly in his chair like one who has given up and is waiting for justice, legal or poetic, to take its course.

After a long silence, a strategy that failed to unnerve Ed, Clive resumed. 'Ed, did you kill Lucy?' His question was gentle rather than confronting.'

'Yes, I suppose I did.' The answer came after another long silence.

'What do you mean you suppose you did?' Ken was annoyed. 'You either did or you didn't!'

Clive shook his head at Ken, as if to say 'go easy'.

'Why, Ed? Why? What made you do it?' Clive had interviewed killers before, the scared, the defiant, the weepers, the ones who enjoyed playing cat-and-mouse believing they could outwit him, but this one left him puzzled.

'Things happen.' Ed's voice could hardly be heard. 'Even when you love someone. It's sometimes hard to say why…'

Ken was angry. They'd got a confession, but he'd been robbed of the opportunity to snare Ed with his cleverness.

Clive got to his feet. He could see little point pressing Ed. He would continue to be evasive or non-committal. There would be time for more answers later.

'You can charge him now,' he said to Ken. 'You've admitted it now, Ed. I'm asking you to write a statement. Will you at least do that for us?'

Ed nodded.

In the days that followed, Ed would give no further reasons, despite Clive's coaxing, and he wouldn't confirm any details. Clive was puzzled. Whatever was his motive? Was it an accident? A sudden moment that could never be taken back and would forever be regretted? He remembered the first interview on the night of the murder when he'd asked Ed whether his marriage was happy. Ed had replied instantly, and he'd believed him. He even remembered thinking of Elizabeth and feeling grateful. There had to be something they didn't know.

Ken thought Clive was too soft with Ed. There was nothing strange about the case, so why was Clive so…so indulgent, but his superior's record spoke for itself.

*

The 7.30 Report was quick to report on the same night as the confession. The ABC opted for more rigorous and balanced reporting than some of the more ill-informed and sensationalist channels. The interviewer, a slim-faced woman with cropped blonde hair and glasses, introduced the celebrated psychologist Dr Curtis Snell. He was a spare man with receding hair, a short greying beard and penetrating grey eyes.

'Doctor, apart from killings committed by radicalised terrorists, a lot has recently been said about domestic violence, and in particular, psychopathic killers. I'm referring of course to the Ed Grainger confession. Can you explain what psychopathy is?'

'Simply put, it's an antisocial personality disorder. Most people see the world in much the same way, but the psychopath sees the world quite differently and has different notions of right and wrong.'

'And how much of this can be explained physiologically?'

'There is some research that indicates the brain of the psychopath is different. Decreased neural activity has been discovered in the paralimbic regions of the brain, the part that controls inhibition, emotions and moral reasoning.'

'What are some of the symptoms that we, without the training you have, might be able to recognise?'

'It's important to understand that the psychopath, and even the psychopathic killer, is an individual, and there may be marked differences between them. They can't all be tarred with the same brush. That said, the most typical sign is a lack of remorse. You may remember that Ted Bundy, who killed over thirty women in the United States, not only didn't feel guilt for anything he'd done, but he felt sorry for those who did.'

'What other signs are there?'

'They tend to lack empathy, have little regard for anyone else, and they are often quite charming, but manipulative. They are always pervasive liars.'

'So what you said before about, what was it, decreased neural activity, does that mean less inhibition, less emotion, at least as we understand it, and less understanding of right and wrong?'

'Generally speaking, yes.'

'Dr Snell, are there any social or home factors that might explain psychopathy?'

'Nothing definitive, though poor parenting may well increase the risk. Of course, while some may have been abused, many come from good families.'

'We've heard a great deal recently about Ed Grainger. I'm sure you've kept abreast of the news. I understand that you would need more time and opportunity to make a valid diagnosis, but in your expert opinion, could Ed Grainger possibly be a psychopathic killer?'

'As you say, I would need the opportunity to interview him. It's dangerous to go labelling people without a thorough analysis. But there are some superficial pointers. He doesn't seem to exhibit any painful feeling of self-reproach, though he seems depressed. He has excelled at lying and manipulation, and the way he conducted the murder was reckless, especially for a supposedly intelligent man. I don't want to be misquoted…but yes, I believe it is probable that he at least has psychopathic tendencies.'

And of course, Dr Snell was misquoted. 'Probably' became 'definitely'.

10

The office was full of congratulation and silent self-congratulation. Ed had confessed and had been charged. He was now incarcerated and awaiting trial. The prosecution was building its case, and Ed had already been assigned a lawyer he didn't want. Headquarters had commended their efforts, and praised them for the way they had coordinated the work of the task force.

The media coverage was extensive. A villain had been caught and justice foreshadowed. The sudden sensation would be massaged for several days to come, before interest would just as quickly die and be forgotten.

All three of them had been praised in media reports, and the commissioner had congratulated them by phone, speaking to each one of them individually, thanking them for restoring the ailing image of the police force. A gag had been imposed on any further talk with the media. The upcoming trial was not to be jeopardised.

They were alone in the office the day after Ed had been taken away. Clive was in his usual position, feet on the desk, deep in thought, Ken was still intent on scanning the newspapers for accolades, occasionally stopping with a 'Listen to this' and reading the praise. Kane sat humbly by the wall. He couldn't believe his good fortune. Only a probationary officer, and he'd already snared recognition for his part in one of the most celebrated cases in Australian criminal history. Sarah was proud of him.

'You deserve the praise, Ken.' Clive was warm yet sober with his compliment.

'Couldn't have done it without you, Clive. They were mainly your ideas.'

'You carried them out,' Clive responded generously, 'and it was your idea to check all the dry cleaners.'

'Thanks, Clive.' He sincerely meant it. 'You cautioned me when I wanted to bring him in after we found the knife. I realise now it was premature. It might not have been enough, and it might have compromised the case against him. And I want to thank you, Kane. I wouldn't mind betting there's a permanent position here if you want it.'

Kane was delighted but self-effacing. 'It was your doing, Ken. You were the commanding officer, and I was simply a foot soldier.'

'I like your humility, Kane,' Clive said. 'You've fitted in really well. You've become a valuable member of the team. I hope you are happy to stay with us.'

'You bet I am. Thanks, Clive. And thank you both for treating me like an equal, and not lording it over me.'

Love all round.

Ken was still basking in the glory. 'Just think of all those hours we spent, interviewing and running checks on all those suspects, and the answer was staring us right in the face. I could hardly believe it. But that's police work, isn't it, Clive? Hard slog, leaving no stone unturned.'

'That interview with Ed…' Clive began reflectively.

'Ed's confession?' Ken queried. 'You handled it well, Clive. That soft touch of yours.'

'Thank you for saying so,' Clive replied. 'It wasn't like any interview I've done before. Ed didn't try to defend himself. Usually when the killer's gone as far as a confession, he's busting for us to understand why he did it. It's a plea to be understood.'

'He might feel that saying nothing doesn't give the prosecution any ammunition,' Ken replied. 'I wouldn't be at all surprised if he retracts his confession before the trial.'

'You could be right.' Clive was uneasy. Something didn't feel right.

*

There was no pleasure for Daniel in hearing the news of Ed's confession.

Lucy had made the wrong choice for a partner. History had proven that in the most appalling way, but a love or deep affection can linger even in an ethos of recrimination. He'd have liked to know why Ed had killed her, but knew that he'd never find the truth. Reasons are like labels. They hide multiple realities. He certainly had no faith in the fictions the press and glossy magazines would peddle to a public hungry for sensation.

Ed was a rival, but an unwitting one. He remembered his own bitterness, his rage when Lucy left him, particularly when he'd given up the chance of a lifetime job to keep her. He wondered if Ed had felt the same anger at that terrible moment when he'd struck, the moment that could never be reclaimed. Perhaps it would haunt him for the rest of his life.

In those early months after the confession, he felt hostility towards Ed for what he'd done, but it was tempered by a certain empathy, and he even considered visiting him one day in gaol. Circumstance had bonded them. But time ate its way into such half-formed plans.

Within two years, he was married to Amelia, a blonde lookalike of Lucy's, and he was equally as infatuated with her as he had been with Lucy. They stayed living happily together in the area, had three children, and enjoyed long lives.

Amelia, who was told of his history with Lucy, was understanding, and was often warned light-heartedly, 'If you ever travel, it will be with me.'

Anne felt a curlicue of pleasure when hearing the news. Lucy had died, but the circumstances of her death, murdered by her husband, proved that she must have suffered in her marriage for some time before that. Even experiencing that twist of pleasure made her feel guilty, and she chided herself. Lucy may have died, been killed in a gruesome way, but to derive pleasure from such a happening was not worthy of her.

She softened in her attitude towards Lucy, a result of her cruel death, though she never fully forgave her. Instead, she transferred her hostility to Bob Ellis. He was the one, after all, who fired her.

She found employment with a rival company, delighting when they secured contracts ahead of her former employers. But she never understood why she kept being overlooked for promotion, and was less than charitable to those who were successful.

Her children, already in their early teens, grew up and married early. One left Australia to live with her husband in Edinburgh. The other moved interstate. They rarely visited. After the marriage of her youngest child, her husband left her. Her retirement was lonely, and her rancour with the world increased, turning to glee when someone was reported and punished for some horrific act.

She remained in the family home until the end, never softening in her view that the world had conspired against her, and died from a stroke in her mid-seventies. Her death was not discovered for months.

'Bloody well serves them right,' Craig told his drinking companions at the pub. He'd been pleased when Lucy had been murdered, and didn't try to hide his feelings. She deserved it. Forgiveness was foreign to him. He'd have made sure she suffered. Mercy might be humility's true badge, but he had no use for such tokens. The satisfaction was doubled when Ed had been charged with her murder. They had been paid for the injustice they inflicted on him. He shouted drinks all round.

It occurred to him that with both of them gone, and the mother dead, he might now have some claim on their wealth. He was the only one left in the bloodline. Surely that entitled him. Ed would probably be in gaol for the rest of his life. There was no, what did the lawyers call it, 'issue', children from the marriage, so he thought he had a legitimate claim. He determined to investigate that likelihood as soon as possible.

Three months later, having failed to have any joy with claiming the Grainger assets, he returned home to find Fern was no longer interested in him, and had found someone else. A week later, he was arrested for armed burglary, and sentenced to eight years. Even as the sentence was imposed, he smiled at the irony that he might confront Ed in gaol, but he was incarcerated elsewhere in a maximum-security prison.

He served his time, with no leniency for good behaviour, as there was no good behaviour, but reoffended within months of his release, and was returned to gaol.

He died in prison in his early forties, the cause of his death shrouded in secrecy. There were several explanations: that he was beaten to death by prison guards, that he was murdered by fellow prisoners, and that he died of a drug overdose or trying to cheat drug lords of their profits. He was so full of himself that suicide was never considered a possibility.

Berice was thought by many to be mad, but she wasn't fickle. Despite the continual rejections that would have discouraged the sanest of people, Ed still held some hold over her affections. She may have entertained thoughts that Ed had murdered Lucy to clear the way for her, but if she did, his arrest and the likelihood of his spending the rest of his life in gaol would have challenged any faint hope she still nursed.

She was saddened but silent when the news of Ed's confession broke, knowing that Derek wouldn't be sympathetic and was going to be watching her curiously, ready to pounce. They never spoke of Ed now, but Derek was plagued for the rest of his life by the knowledge she'd experienced something special with Ed that she'd never felt for him.

Even though Derek had been charged with the assault of Ed, he took no particular pleasure from Ed's confession and charging. He greeted many of the surprises life threw up with a mute fascination and incomprehension. The only words he spoke to Berice about Ed's capture were a rare form of praise for Ed: 'He's got more balls than I thought.'

Husband and wife stayed together through the years, their limited minds united by their shared impotence. They quarrelled incessantly but were mutually dependent, and became the bane of the local council for hoarding every imaginable form of rubbish that was left metres deep in the front yard, and in every room of the house. They had no children, lived long lives, and died within a month of each other in the same nursing home.

*

Adrian was the last to hear of Ed's confession. He'd been late home from a conference of the law fraternity when the news broke the previous night, and on the way to work the following morning, he'd opted for a soothing Beethoven CD rather than the car radio. It had been a merry night.

Stella had been too self-absorbed to share the news. She had argued with Letitia, a not unusual occurrence, asking her to help clear up after breakfast, and Letitia, a not atypical nine-year-old girl, had thrown a tantrum, shouting and stamping her feet.

'All the girls are ganging up on me,' a non sequitur, 'and you're no help at all. You don't care!'

'Not true.' Adrian had placed a calming hand on her shoulder as he headed for the door on his way to work, and was grateful to leave the rest of the pacifying to Stella.

'Good morning Adrian.' Blanche's cultured voice was all sweetness. Her anonymous call to the police about Lucy and her boss hadn't been revealed, and she could relax. She knew now that it wouldn't be mentioned at the trial. It wasn't part of the evidence. Lucy was no longer a threat, or rival, and she could never be certain what she'd heard in Adrian's office that evening when she'd returned for her glasses. Perhaps it was her vivid imagination. Or anxiety. She had taken no pleasure in Lucy's death.

'Morning,' Adrian replied, having hurried from the underground car park. He was feeling buoyant. He'd re-established old links and made new ones at the conference.

'What about last night's news?' Blanche said, wide-eyed and expectant as he entered, waiting for the pleasure of sharing startling information.

'Late night,' Adrian said. 'Missed the news. I'll catch up now,' and he waved the folded newspaper he'd bought on the way to work.

He entered his office and closed the door, not noticing Blanche's disappointment, put his briefcase in its customary place, and threw the paper on his desk, where it landed face-up. The conspicuous lettering caught his eye and he sat down in slow motion, his eyes drawn to the bold headlines reporting Ed Grainger's confession.

'Bloody hell,' he said aloud, and reached for the intercom with a trembling hand. 'Would you cancel my first appointment, Blanche, and reschedule.'

'You've read…' she began.

'Just reschedule,' he said tersely.

He sat down, spread the newspaper on his desk and read the relevant parts. Then he stood up from the high-backed leather chair at his desk, and moved slowly to the windows, where he stood with his hands in his pockets watching the stream of traffic from the tenth floor, and the workers scurrying like ants into the nearby office buildings. The intercom sounded.

'Your coffee, Adrian?' Blanche was hesitant.

'Leave it,' he said testily, and moved to his chair, still muttering. 'What the hell!'

Blanche knew he'd now seen the headlines, perhaps read about the weight of evidence that forced Ed's confession, the knife and the dry-cleaned shirt. She couldn't wait to observe his reaction, to meet her friends and retail the gossip, to share their tut-tut wonder at the depravity of humanity.

Adrian shook his head, looked at the newspaper again, sat down, and took fifteen minutes to read the first four pages, all devoted to Ed's confession and the impressive police work that had unravelled the crime, the near-impossible discovery of the knife and the dry-cleaned shirt.

'Why? Why?' His lawyer's brain grappled to explain it. It couldn't be some sort of elaborate game. Or could it? What did Ed Grainger think he was doing? He must know confession meant a life sentence.

Perplexed, he sat for several minutes. Thoughts jostled for ascendancy in his mind. He looked at the framed and crocheted plaque on the wall opposite, given to him when he graduated, reading, 'Where laws end, tyranny begins.' The several minutes of thought didn't give him an answer. He smiled quizzically, arranged the papers into neat piles on his desk, a token of order in a chaotic world, and buzzed Blanche.

'I'll have that coffee now,' he said brightly. 'And Blanche, sorry if I was a bit short with you before. I do appreciate all you do. And could you ring Stella and tell her I'll be home early.'

He hadn't been unduly worried, but you never could tell. Sometimes there were diaries from which a story could be pieced together, or a conscience-stricken witness wondering whether to come forward. But he was certainly safe now! He'd incinerated his bloodied shirt the following day, watched it turn to ashes, even removed the charred buttons from his backyard incinerator. And he'd dropped the knife overboard, a kilometre out to sea.